TOWER ISLAND
W
E
PAGOS ISLAN
rage
LITTLE PAL
NTA
RUZ
PALMELO
SANTA FE
Wreck of the Black Jack
SAN CRISTOBAL
SANTA MARIA
GARDNER
ESPANOLA

GREEN SAILORS IN
THE GALAPAGOS

The crew of *Rag Doll II* set sail for the Galapagos
Islands in response to a mysterious letter from an
old shipmate of Uncle George.

GREEN SAILORS IN THE GALAPAGOS

by

Gilbert Hackforth-Jones

Illustrated by
Jean Main and David Cobb, R.O.I.

LONDON
HODDER AND STOUGHTON

*The characters in this book are
entirely imaginary and bear no relation
to any living person*

*Made and Printed in Great Britain for
Hodder and Stoughton Limited, London,
by Cox & Wyman Limited, London,
Fakenham and Reading*

FOREWORD

This is a story of what happened to the Green Sailors when first they entered the mighty Pacific Ocean.

The Galapagos Islands, or Colon Archipelago, may be found in any atlas but the reader will have some difficulty in identifying Palmelo and Little Palmelo islands—for they do not exist in the form described in this book. All the animals, birds, reptiles and insects are real characters. Colonel Gaspardo, the Chief of Police of San Cristobal, is not and was not, as far as I know, in existence.

G. H-J.

St. George's Day.
23 April 1959.

CONTENTS

CONTENTS

ILLUSTRATIONS

Chapter One

IT ALL DEPENDS ON WHAT YOU MEAN BY "SUPERLATIVELY RICH"

THE Air Port at Parham, Antigua, was a pretty primitive affair, a legacy of the war left by the United States Air Forces. It consisted mainly of a long strip of concrete, a small pavilion-like building, and a wind-sock. The great bird-like plane swooped down to the landing—some half a dozen passengers disembarked and their seats were quickly snapped up by an equal number who had been waiting for many days for the chance to obtain transport.

Before the new arrivals had been released by the Customs and Immigration authorities the aeroplane was on its way again, making a journey of minutes where *Rag Doll* would have taken hours as it hopped from strip to strip down the Windward and Leeward islands to its ultimate destination— at Trinidad.

Waiting at the Airport in a state of impatience difficult to conceal was Uncle George who had driven there in his new car to meet Herr Gustavus, a diamond merchant who had flown from Amsterdam at Uncle George's urgent request to negotiate the purchase of the diamonds.

Readers of *Green Sailors in the Caribbean* will, I trust, forgive me for recapitulating briefly the circumstances which caused me to end the last chronicle with the words—"and superlatively rich", for the sake of those who have not read that story.

After a series of near-disasters, discoveries and an escape

from Bird Island in the partly dismasted *Rag Doll* the Greens, Ted Tottle, Loopy Lomas and Polly-the-Parrot were making their way towards the distant island of Antigua when an orange-coloured balloon was sighted, bobbing placidly on the surface of the sullen waters, still under the waning influence of the recent hurricane.

From their discovery of the base at Bird Island they knew already that this balloon could have started its journey in the nose-cone of the rocket which they had seen fired the previous night—the self-same rocket whose trajectory had been disturbed by the explosion aboard the schooner *Rattlesnake*. And they knew (or thought they knew) that attached to this balloon would be a parcel of diamonds originally destined to be fired into the waiting hands of accomplices off the island of Vieques (or Crab Island). Amid great excitement Loopy Lomas, that insouciant young Canadian, had dived overboard and recovered the balloon. Their most fervent hopes were fulfilled when the leather bag, attached to the balloon was opened, and handfuls of glittering gems revealed themselves. This, together with their reunion with Uncle George who was subsequently lowered on to *Rag Doll* from a helicopter after a worrying search for his beloved *Rag Doll* and her crew, brought their most exciting adventure to a successful conclusion. No further troubles were experienced and they reached the historic little haven of English Harbour without difficulty. There, with the assistance of the local ship-repairers, they set about rerigging *Rag Doll* and were joined immediately by Captain and Mrs. Green, the parents, who had flown direct to Antigua from England.

This sudden acquisition of wealth might well have caused everybody to lose their heads, and to a small extent it did. In this they were encouraged by the local tradespeople who were exceedingly anxious to provide them with all that was needed until such time as the diamonds, now safely lodged at a Bank, could be turned into cash. Uncle George had allowed himself the luxury of a nice little shooting-brake, a necessity on an island where there is little public transport. Ted had settled on a valuable movie-camera. Loopy Lomas's eyes kept straying to a handy little five-tonner, lying in the harbour. He was in two minds, was Loopy, whether to continue to sail with his friends or to chance his arm single-handed among the many attractive islands of the Caribbean, or rather he *had* been in two minds until Uncle George made his astonishing announcement. Uncle George had been in solemn conclave with Captain and Mrs. Green for several days before agreement had been reached. Many arguments had taken place with the long-suffering parents of the Green Sailors: cunning ones by Uncle George, pointing out the wonderful broadening influence of world travel: common-sense ones by Mrs. Green, pointing out that education in the rudiments of the arts and sciences must not be neglected, which it might well be if her children were allowed to continue to live aboard *Rag Doll*. "What about Ted Tottle?" Uncle George had asked. He was a trained schoolmaster, well qualified to take them all through a proper curriculm. "Where?" asked Captain Green. "At sea", Uncle George had replied. "How much education have the children received during their recent voyage across the Atlantic?" asked Captain Green. Ted was sent for and gave a fairly satisfactory answer. The parents went away by themselves to discuss the pros and cons of turning their children loose for yet another long period. It was a difficult decision to make. They were naturally very fond of the Green Sailors: to say yes to Uncle George's proposals would be to deprive themselves of the company of their own children for many more months. On the other hand an opportunity such as now presented itself might never again occur: besides there was no denying that the Green Sailors had flourished in their life of hardship, danger and high adventure. Mark now had a steady look in his eyes which men prize above all else. He had faced dangers, and had taken decisions, he had developed his body-muscles and was now as strong as a horse. Mary, ever sensible, had a sparkle in her eyes which told its own tale—she, too was a hardened traveller, the sort which in the past spread the English breed all over the world, to its lasting betterment.

As for Binnie and Ben, they too were thriving, Binnie especially. They were like a couple of well-trained shooting-dogs, ready to move at speed on the word of command and content with very little entertainment when life entered into one of its more humdrum periods. "The proof"—said Captain Green, as if coining a new phrase—"of the pudding is in the eating." He was very proud of his four youngsters and grateful to Uncle George for all he had done and was doing for them. Yet, there was no denying that they'd been subjected to a great deal of danger.

Far into the night the parents debated. In the morning they had decided.

"You can take them," said the Father, "on condition that you don't go looking for trouble and that they do at least four hours' "school" every day."

The Green Sailors had been pretty well aware of what was being debated for Uncle George had given himself away numerous times: for example he had cabled to London for a monumental supply of charts, and that could only mean one thing. He had also been debating the desirability of carrying a small distillation plant for making fresh water from salt. He had given a large order for canned foods, and the sail-makers of Falmouth (Antigua) were duplicating *Rag Doll*'s entire outfit of sails. Clearly Uncle George was going to spend his share of the diamond money on an extensive cruise—the question was—with whom?

When Captain Green calmly announced that he had decided to allow them to continue the voyage ROUND THE WORLD they could scarcely believe their ears. They crowded round their parents trying to express their delight at the prospect and their sorrow at having once again to say good-bye: in this latter act they were not quite so successful. After all, they reasoned, if they were not to have gone sailing they would by now have been banished to boarding-school for three-quarters of the year.

Since the Hurricane season was now fully in operation, however, there was no great haste required in the refitting of *Rag Doll*. To show their gratitude further the Greens settled down to full days of schooling in one of the old offices in Nelson's dockyard into which they had moved while workmen were repairing the water tanks. It was hot and rather monotonous work after the happy-go-lucky life of the past months but the reward was clearly to be seen, like a carrot before a donkey's nose. Ted Tottle was a good teacher and there was plenty of time left to play, chiefly in the water, or on the water, and to go spring-gun shooting for turtles and other large fish, in which for a few weeks they were joined by their parents until Captain and Mrs. Green were obliged to fly away back to England to do the work from which they had taken this delightful holiday.

Herr Johannes Gustavus of Amsterdam, the diamond merchant, was a small man. He walked slowly and always spoke with quiet deliberation. His manner was that of a family doctor visiting a patient whom he suspects to be malingering.

After he had shaken hands with Uncle George and seated

himself beside him in the shooting-brake he observed that he hoped that Uncle George would not be disappointed with the result of his valuation of the diamonds. The price of these gems, he said, was purely artificial, the market at the present moment was depressed by the prospect of universal peace. It required wars and rumours of wars, he explained, to send up the price of diamonds. That was when far-seeing people sold their stocks and shares and bought things which were imperishable.

Uncle George, who hadn't been born yesterday listened with amused interest to Herr Gustavus's preamble—this was what was called "softening-up" talk—to prepare the owner of the gems for a small bid for them. It is a common enough commercial practice, especially in anything to do with second-hand goods. Clearly Herr Gustavus was a keen business-man. Uncle George prepared for a mighty tussle, as he drove carefully into the town of St. John's, Antigua, through roads and streets littered with cyclists, children, donkeys and fowls.

At the Bank they were greeted with great respect, as befitted such rich depositors, and ushered into an airy room. Then the Manager retired to the strong-room and returned shortly afterwards with that leather bag which has travelled by so many routes since leaving the rich diamond mines of the Congo. Stolen goods these probably were, and if it could be proved that they belonged to the Diamond Corporation, this organisation had already expressed its gratitude to Uncle George by waiving all claim. The diamonds were his and now the question was—how much were they worth?

When the Manager had withdrawn Uncle George broke the seal which the Bank had placed on the string which secured the neck of the bag, and poured a heap of glittering jewels on to the table.

18

Herr Gustavus fixed a magnifying glass in his eye and with a practised hand picked up diamond after diamond with a small pair of forceps and carefully examined each one, while Uncle George lit his pipe and tried to restrain his impatience. There was something maddeningly irritating in the way in which the expert went about his business; he neither spoke nor showed by his expression what was passing through his mind. As he worked he was dividing the collection into two heaps—one of which was far greater than the other. When at last he had completed the sorting out process he looked up at the expectant watcher and sighed gently.

"The big heap," he said, "not very good, not good at all. The little heap pretty fair."

Uncle George swallowed hard. He had an uncomfortable feeling that he was dealing with an honest man who was not enjoying his task.

"I see," he said, puffing a huge smoke-ring to hide his discomfiture. "Well, let's hear the worst!"

"In English money," said Herr Gustavus, "seven hundred pounds."

The words sounded a knell in the heart of his listener. Seven hundred pounds would not go far to pay the air-passages of the Green parents, the new mast and sails—and the further expenses expected on the Round-the-World trip.

"Are you quite sure?" he asked.

Herr Gustavus shrugged his shoulders. "Within a few pounds, but of course I will submit them to further examination by my colleagues and if they disagree then I will adjust the price."

He took out his cheque-book and began to write, and while he did so Uncle George began to think what this would mean to his gallant band—the abandonment of the world trip, the disappointment of all—and his own financial difficulties arising out of his somewhat reckless counting of his chickens before the eggs were hatched. It did not spell ruin or anything like that but it was a hearty smack between the eyes and required a lot of self-control on his part not to show his great disappointment.

"I won't deny that I expected a great deal more", he said.

"I was afraid of that," said Herr Gustavus; "it was but natural. People are always inclined to over-value any jewels which they come by. Human cupidity eh?" He smiled and carefully scanned the cheque before blotting it. "Before leaving Amsterdam I received instructions to purchase these stones at the market price"—he paused and then went on deliberately—"*plus* a small additional figure which was to be adjusted according to the value of these diamonds. I trust you will find it satisfactory?"

He held out the cheque. Uncle George had again to exercise iron restraint as he took the piece of paper and fumbled for his reading spectacles. He was not going to allow this foreign gentleman to witness his disappointment. Hardly bothering to read the figures on the cheque he began to fold it.

"I shall require a receipt", said Herr Gustavus gently. "In fact two receipts—one for seven hundred pounds and the other for five thousand."

"Good gracious!" Uncle George held the cheque before his startled eyes. "That's deuced generous!"

"I think not", said the Dutch gentleman. "I did my best to obtain more, but business is business. Will it, in fact reimburse you for all your expenditure? If not I can but try to obtain more."

Uncle George swallowed again. He felt like dancing a jig and embracing this nice little man who liked to write cheques for thousands instead of hundreds. His troubles had vanished. All his debts would be paid. His crew would be able to indulge themselves (though Loopy would have to forego his dream-ship) and best of all there would be enough over for his treasured project.

Hastily he took his pen and wrote out the receipts with a slightly trembling hand.

"I am perfectly satisfied", he said, as he handed them over.

"You have omitted to apply the four-cent stamps", said Herr Gustavus. "Kindly do so and sign across them."

Chapter Two

LETTER FROM THE GALAPAGOS ISLANDS

THE exploits of the Green Sailors in the Caribbean had not gone unnoticed by the World press. Their discovery of the diamond smuggler's method of shooting the gems into the U.S.A. by means of rockets was sensational enough, and the fact that this had been effected by a crew whose average age was well under twenty was just what the newspapers liked to feature. "Teenage Heroes!" went the headlines. Photographs of the entire crew, plus, of course Polly-the-Parrot appeared everywhere. Even Uncle George who, through no fault of his own, had played a minor role in the operation was given what nowadays is called "A Profile"; this ought to have meant that his silhouette was on display but didn't: it was simply that his life-story and characteristics were described in intimate detail.

Odd-looking journalists were always descending from the skies and going away again with various sidelights on the story, according to whether they had interviewed Binnie (blood-thirsty), Ted (taciturn) Loopy (loquacious), or Uncle George (accurate).

Tape-recordings of their interviews went out on the various radio networks to reach the far ends of the earth, so that lonely trappers in the Yukon, pearl-fishers in the Maldive Islands, harpoonists in the South Atlantic, and even listeners to the Third Programme in Bloomsbury were given a vivid description of the episode. In this age news travels everywhere where there is enough electricity to operate a listening set, and with the development of the solar battery anybody who now lives where the sun shines most of the time can capture enough energy to be able to listen to the doings of the outside world; the farther away from civilisation such people are, moreover, the more they listen to the messages which crowd the ether in every language, and on every topic.

Thus it was not suprising that a considerable "fan-mail" began to pour into the Post Office Box in St. Johns, Antigua from all over the world. Many such letters were written by people who thought it would be a good idea if the Green Sailors parted with some of the wealth which they were reputed to have acquired. Some were frankly enthusiastic about the courage and ingenuity shown by the young people and wrote to say so. Some were disapproving of the parents and uncle of the children for allowing them to get into such scrapes.

Others were from old friends and acquaintances who just wanted to write and say hello! It was mostly great fun opening the letters and answering them, for every one unpleasantly worded missive there would be ten or more which were well meant. These were answered in suitable terms of gratitude; the others were ignored.

Of all the many dozens which Uncle George received personally the one which interested him most came from one of the Galapagos Islands—an archipelago some eight hundred miles south-west of the Panama Canal and directly on the line of the route planned by him in his forthcoming Round-the-World trip. To find an old shipmate in such an out-of-the-world spot as Palmelo Island from which the letter was addressed was exciting in itself, for every traveller knows that it adds a great deal to the pleasures of arrival to be able to call on someone who will give you a warm welcome. It was a long letter and beautifully typewritten and ran as follows:

"My dear Commander Firebrace, (this was Uncle George's surname).

"You probably do not remember me as well as I do you, but perhaps the mention of H.M.S. *Borealis* in the China Seas before the last war will stir a chord in your memory? I was the most junior of all Surgeon-Lieutenants aboard the good ship and you, if I remember rightly, were a Submarine Captain doing what you used to call your "big ship penance". I had a bad time in the war, having been picked up, more dead than alive, by a Japanese warship after the *Doris* was sunk in action with her. As the result of this and subsequent misfortunes as a P.O.W. I was invalided out of the Service and given to understand that I had but a short time to live. This somewhat rash prophecy on the part of my medical colleagues was fortunately untrue, and I am now as fit as a flea (with one eye), and this explains my presence on this otherwise uninhabited island: *Palmelo* it is called—some twenty miles north-west of San Cristobal, a perfect paradise of an island if you don't mind being eaten alive by mosquitoes! I am here as a volunteer on behalf of the Christopherson Research Foundation, to observe and catalogue the numerous birds and beasts for which this Archipelago has been famous ever since Charles Darwin visited it in the *Beagle* all those years ago.

"It's a lonely life but it suits me, or rather it did suit me until I tuned in my radio the other day and heard your cheerful voice describing the almost unbelievable adventures of your nephews and nieces in the Caribbean. I also heard (and correct me if I'm wrong) you mention your plans for continuing your journey, after rest and refreshment, right round the world, via the usual stopping places, which of course must include these islands. That being so I shall regard it as an act of friendship if you will pay me a visit at Palmelo, bringing with you the attached list of stores, and, more important still some books. I have now read the works of Jane Austen fifteen times and can recite whole chunks of them. Especially please remember the D.D.T.

My term on this island is due to last another six months, by which time I will have collected enough biological specimens and made observations of the seasonal changes in the animal life of this place. I shall then return to the C.R.F. Headquarters in San Francisco via Ecuador—not a very pleasant journey with tiresome officialdom at every stage.

"I am greatly enjoying myself but won't deny that the sound of your voice brought back to me the memory of many past pleasures in the good old *Borealis*. After the war I felt I needed solitude and I've certainly had a basinful of it here. And now I am extremely well and anxious to resume a more gregarious life. A visit from you and those entertaining youngsters of yours round about Christmas would just about set me up, and besides there is something you could do for me which would be of benefit to both of us. I am sending this letter via the trading schooner from Guayaquil and it should reach you well before you recommence your journeyings, for I cannot believe that a seasoned mariner such as yourself will set out until the hurricane season is well and truly past. I would like to write on a certain matter in further detail but in these parts where letters are frequently opened in the sacred name of Customs and Excise, not to mention National Security, I dare not. This much I will say—it will be worth your while to pay your old shipmate a visit, and not only for the purpose of renewing our friendship.

"I must close now for I have to take my motor-boat some twenty miles to Bahia Wreck in order to post this letter and

25

to provision-up for a further month or two. You will be amazed at this place: there is nothing like it anywhere on earth, and I am sure your nephews, nieces and the rest of your fascinating crew will be enthralled by what they see here. Be sure to come and don't forget the D.D.T.! I will reimburse you fully when we meet.

"Yours very sincerely,
"Thomas Huntingdon.

"P.S. If you have changed your mind and are not continuing the voyage, please let me know as quickly as possible and I will try to get in touch with someone else. This is pretty important. I wish I could say more but I dare not. T.H."

Uncle George read the letter through several times, racking his brains to try and conjure up from the distant past the memory of Surgeon-Lieutenant Tom Huntingdon. Although, however, he succeeded in checking from an old diary that there had been such an officer in the *Borealis* he could not for the life of him recapture a visual memory of him. Was he the young fellow who sported a beard? No, that had been the Paymaster-Lieutenant. Memory is a fickle sense; it is said that service in the Far East has a bad effect on it. In Uncle George's case he was well aware of whole blanks which he could not fill, while his recollections of other incidents and people of the same period were as vivid as the day when he had experienced them. No, he wouldn't have known Tom Huntingdon if he had been able to slip back in time those twenty years, and as for the present-day version of the ex-Surgeon-Lieutenant, he would only know him from Adam by the facts that he was likely to be wearing more clothes and had apparently lost the sight of one eye. Apart from that, however, it was a most encouraging thought that eagerly waiting on the other side of the Panama Canal, alone on a little island was a man who would

26

be delighted to show the *Rag Doll*'s crew something of the life of the Galapagos Islands, and it would be a trivial act of charity to load the modest list of stores and books which Huntingdon had asked for.

Only one thing in the letter from Palmelo Island gave him food for thought. That was the note of urgency in the postscript. Captain Green had made it a condition that Uncle George was not to get involved in any further adventures, such as those that resulted from allowing himself to be used by the Diamond Corporation. What was it that Huntingdon considered to be "pretty important"? And why was he afraid to come straight out with it on paper?

One thing was quite certain. If Huntingdon wanted *Rag Doll* to help him in something nefarious there would be nothing doing. Still, there would be no harm in paying him a visit.

Chapter Three

THROUGH THE PANAMA CANAL AND WESTWARD HO!

THE great sliding door of the first Gatun lock closed behind *Rag Doll* with a swift and almost noiseless finality. Everyone onboard the ketch recognised the full significance of the closing of that gate. The Atlantic Ocean and all that it meant was irrevocably shut off; ahead of them, behind that other massive door which towered above them was the first of three gigantic steps by which they would climb to reach the summit of the Panama Isthmus: further on they would descend again by another series of locks and so out into the Gulf of Panama and the great Pacific Ocean beyond.

There is always something fascinating about a canal; whether it be one of those narrow inland waterways which criss-cross every country in Europe, regardless of mountainous conditions, or whether it be a giant ship-canal by means of which the largest vessels in the world can "walk" across the land, making use of the simplest of all Archimedian principles to raise and lower themselves. At the entrance to the most extraodinary feat of engineering the world has ever seen, the *Rag Doll*'s crew would not have been human if they had been otherwise than deeply excited, for there, before their very eyes, was concrete evidence in the shape of the high lock walls and the large iron gate from which little gouts of water were gushing to fall with echoing splashes on to the dark surface of the water at the bottom of the lock, that they had indeed finished with the western hemisphere in which hitherto they all had lived. Behind that door were the waters of the Caribbean, for which they had no particular love, beyond them the good clean ocean which stretched back to the shores of Europe and Africa, and up towards the Polar regions where lay their little fog-girt native land in the worst weather and the best climate in the world.

This feeling of the final closing of a chapter in their lives was accentuated by the tremendous echoing effect of lying at the bottom of this forty-foot pit. Above heads they could just see the gangs of workmen who were tending *Rag Doll's* lines. A short distance ahead of the yacht lay a large liner whose passengers crowded aft to look on the British boat which had been front-page news some three months earlier.

There was another reason for recognising the importance of the occasion and one of which Uncle George was particularly aware: *Rag Doll* was now at last beyond the reach of possible enemies, of which there were undoubtedly a large number. Her accidental discovery of the rocket-site on Bird Island had resulted in the complete break-up of the largest criminal organisation in existence. Hundreds of thousands of dollars, pounds, francs and pesos belonging to smugglers had been wiped out as the result of *Rag Doll's* intervention; many people, including the crew of the submarine had been captured, tried and imprisoned, but many more had escaped the round-up. These were not likely to have forgotten to whom they owed their misfortunes.

Uncle George had been warned to be on the look-out for evildoers by Commander Fenton, who had been in charge of the campaign against the smugglers, and knew more about them than anyone else. It had been a secret between the two men; no other member of *Rag Doll's* crew had been aware of certain precautions taken to put any revengeful pursuers off the track. Isolated as they had been in the old Dockyard of English Harbour Antigua, they had not seen the newspapers from both sides of the Atlantic. If they had they would have been surprised to have read that they were sailing for New Orleans where they were to spend Christmas, and that their Round-the-World trip had been abandoned. To make assurance doubly sure Uncle George had sailed from Antigua at dead of night, fully a week before his widely advertised date of departure, and it was not an accident that during the 1,400 mile voyage from Antigua to the entrance to the Canal never a day passed without an aircraft of the U.S. Navy dropping out of the skies to take a quick look at the yacht. Commander Fenton was a conscientious man. He too breathed a heavy sigh of relief when he heard that *Rag Doll* was safely behind the lock-gate. From now on she would be no further concern of his.

In a small back room in New Orleans two disappointed men read of the arrival in the Canal of the vessel they had planned to destroy at the entrance of the Mississippi, and then, being realists they consigned the *Rag Doll* and all her crew to the Devil and turned to other nefarious matters. As far as they were concerned the incident was closed. "No doubt," said one of them: "no doubt we will remember," and having said that they both promptly forgot the whole affair.

Yes, Uncle George had much to be relieved about. From now on he hoped that his only potential dangers would be natural ones. The violence of the sea was always preferable to the hostile acts of human-beings.

Up on the dockside a man dressed in a white suit and wearing, appropriately enough, a Panama hat, hailed Uncle George in an unmistakable American voice.

"Hey you there," he said, "get some warps out to the

other side of the lock and look alive! When we turn on the faucets this bath is going to get rough!" As he spoke two Panamanian riggers hurled their heaving-lines with great accuracy across the bows and stern of the yacht. Quickly the Green Sailors attached a warp to each of them. These were hauled across to the opposite side of the lock so that now *Rag Doll* was held by her four "corners" in midstream. Five minutes later they all saw the necessity of such a precaution.

"Panama Hat" put a whistle to his lips. A steady humming sound started up in the great pump-house on the lock-side and then the still and placid waters of the lock went mad. Water was being admitted through gigantic sluice-valves to fill the lock, and so to float the vessels in it to the level of the next one. Since time was money and the Americans were always very much aware of this truism the speed at which the water entered the lock was such that the surface was turned into a boiling maelstrom. *Rag Doll* was tossed about like an empty egg-shell, but thanks to the four warps which the gangers ashore were keeping taut as she floated upwards on the rapidly rising waters, she came to no harm, though she fretted like an impatient mustang under the influence of the swirling currents.

In an amazingly short space of time the great thousand-foot long and hundred-and-ten-foot-wide lock filled up completely, and in so doing lifted the great liner and the diminutive *Rag Doll* a full thirty feet. "Going up in an elevator," said Loopy, "has nothing on this."

Then the gate ahead of them, which before the lock was flooded had towered so mightily above them, slid back disclosing number two lock, another forty-foot pit similar in all respects to number one. Another whistle from "Panama Hat" and the great liner began slowly to enter the second lock, not under her own power but by half a dozen small engines (or "mules" as they were called), each with a towing warp attached to the ship. When the mules had done their work the gangers attending *Rag Doll*, acting as human mules walked her into the second lock, and when the great door had closed behind her, the whole process of flooding-up was repeated until it was possible to enter the top lock which gave access to the level of the great artificial Gatun Lake.

At this stage Mister Corcoran, a jolly Irish-American canal pilot, came aboard and took control of the yacht. He was delighted to have been selected for the job, he said; usually he had to pilot great cargo-vessels and this was a heavy responsibility, for the waterways across the Panama Isthmus though wide enough for the purpose, seem to be very narrow from the bridge of a twenty-thousand-ton ship. Paddy Corcoran was determined to enjoy his forty-five-mile trip. With Uncle George at the wheel he had nothing to do but to lie full length across the top of *Rag Doll*'s deck-house under the shade of her mainsail, and to talk to his new-found friends. And how he talked! He was a real canal man was Paddy. Born within the sight of it, of parents who had lived and worked there ever since the great work had begun in earnest. He remembered, he said, as a little boy being hoisted on his Father's shoulder to see the first ship in the world to travel from one ocean to another by means of this water bridge, for that was what this waterway really was. By means of dams the entire centre of the narrow neck of land joining the two continents of North and South America had been converted into a huge deep-water lake, through which the largest ships in the world could ply at full speed. At either end of this waterway were the locks, through three of which *Rag Doll* had already passed. Now with a favouring breeze and the diesel engine helping, the ketch moved purposefully on her way towards the Pacific

Ocean while her crew sucked ice-lollies and behaved as though they hadn't a care in the world. Paddy waved frantically to the pilots of all the other ships which kept passing and overtaking and declared his intention of buying a yacht too, and travelling round the world. He was most enthusiastic about the way everything worked aboard *Rag Doll*, and even stopped talking to hear the story of the diamond-smugglers first hand from Binnie.

So passed that historic day as they went across the bridge, through the great Gaillard Cut which had almost caused the failure of the Canal as the sides caved in as fast as the Channel was excavated. Even then, over forty years since the job was completed, the dredgers and excavators were at it removing the silt, and gradually the notorious danger point of the Canal. Then, with the suddenness of the tropics, the sun dropped into the Atlantic Ocean and darkness covered the earth, but not the Canal. Hundreds of great lamps lit the whole place and turned it all into a fairy-land of dark water which sparkled with rays of silver light. Great ships flood-lit and with bands playing on deck were seldom out of sight. This was the highway which connected the two hemispheres. Paddy was proud of it, and kept on saying so.

Soon the next locks were reached, the descent of which was as peaceful as the ascent had been turbulent. It was like pulling the plug out of a bath—the water level dropped so rapidly that they had a sense of falling. Down into the echoing pits—through the doors and out finally into the broad and placid waters of La Boca in the Gulf of Panama, and in the mighty Pacific Ocean—the greatest of them all and, so they were told—the friendliest.

What sort of adventures awaited them in those thousands of miles ahead?

Chapter Four

CONVERGING COURSES

*R*AG DOLL spent several days in port after leaving the
Canal, during which time the final provisioning for the
long haul across the Pacific Ocean was carried out with the
greatest care. It would be all of four thousand miles' sailing to
the west before it would again be possible to walk into a ship-
chandler's office and order anything and everything needed
in a ship. Extra fuel drums were taken aboard, for the
weather during the next four hundred miles was likely to be
too calm for sailing and the diesel engine would have to be
used until the vicinity of the Trade Winds could be reached.
Uncle George's distillation plant was awaiting him at Balboa,
having been flown out to him from England. It was a neat
little contrivance which burned oil (another reason for
taking extra fuel). It boiled the salt water from the sea and
condensed the steam, leaving the salt behind in the first
chamber. Though it was small it could be guaranteed to
produce enough drinking water for every member of the
crew, and that was a great comfort. No doubt there would
be enough rainfall to keep *Rag Doll* well supplied, but you
never knew—the time might come when this gadget would
come in handy. Until then it was stowed away in the after-
store, along with the fuel drums.

It was stiflingly hot in Panama and everyone was anxious
to be gone, but Uncle George was taking as few chances as
possible. One of his tasks was to go to the Ecuadorian Con-
sulate to obtain a special permit to visit the Galapagos which,

because of the rarity of the animals, birds and reptiles on the islands had been made a game-preserve, and no one was allowed to land there without a permit to do so. It was hot and tiresome work, waiting in offices for officials who were never immediately ready to receive a visitor, who in no circumstances would hurry and who liked to ask a great number of questions, and not only to ask—to write them down in triplicate, together with Uncle George's answers. After several visits, at long last an official document was handed over in return for a considerable sum of money, and *Rag Doll* was free to depart. Before sailing, Uncle George penned a short letter to Tom Huntingdon, informing him of his intended visit to Palmelo Island. This would reach its destination in one of the regular trading schooners which ply between the mainland and the islands. There would be plenty of time for Tom Huntingdon to prepare the Christmas feast which the Green Sailors had decided to celebrate with him, taking with them plenty of tinned turkey, puddings, crackers and nuts. It would be an odd sensation to spend Christmas on the Equator, with never a chance of waking up to see the world turned white and no possible mail from home with its dozens of cards and presents from friends and relatives. Somewhere in the distant future a large sack of letters and parcels would be waiting for them all. Until then they must be content to send and receive short messages by their small radio-transmitter, or by a passing steamer. That was one of the prices (and a heavy one) which these voyagers would have to pay for their freedom of the seas. Christmas, so far from home, would be likely to make them think of those whom they had left behind. The party with Tom Huntingdon would do a great deal to fend off their feelings of homesickness, thought Uncle George.

As things turned out his precautions were not entirely

successful. Christmas in the Galapagos was not certain to be a merry one, for already another party unknown to the Green Sailors were steering a converging course and were destined to meet them on Palmelo Island.

They were Captain Hooker, skipper of the fifty-ton schooner *Black Jack*, "Cobbo" an Australian, "Fatso" an American citizen, and Pedro Gonzalez an Ecuadorian. With names such as these one would have expected the *Black Jack* to be flying the Jolly Roger, and with some justification, for they were an oddly assorted bunch. Whether they were actually crooks, in the sense that they had ever been found out, is hard to say except in one instance, but the fact that they were all at sea and far from their native lands indicates that they were of a roving disposition. So of course, were the Green Sailors and the rest of their crew, but these four men were different. They had sailed from a South American port with a definite object in view; they had no permit to visit the islands, but that wasn't worrying them much. They knew what they wanted and the reward that awaited them if they accomplished their mission. What did worry them was that they hadn't been long at sea in each others' company before they discovered that not one of them was half the sea-faring gentleman he'd made himself out to be. Certainly Captain Jeff Hooker had been in the Merchant Navy, and had been an officer—what he omitted to tell his employer was that he had been a purser with all the knowledge in the world of cargo and financial business, but *none* of deep-sea navigation. "Cobbo" (or to give him his real name for once—Rob Crewdson) had also lied about his technical knowledge. He certainly had been round the world half a dozen times, but one doesn't learn much navigation as a greaser in the engine-room of a tramp steamer.

"Fatso" (Arbuckle) had boasted of his record in the U.S. Air Force. According to him he was the lad who had directed General Doolittle in the first atom-bomb raid. He had also many years earlier been the man who had taught Lindberg (the first single-handed aviator to fly the Atlantic) about navigation. That might have been true, for Lindberg knew little or none; he just aimed at Europe and hit France, a good enough shot in the circumstances.

As for Gonzalez, he'd been brought along because of his knowledge of the language and the fact that he had once lived in one of the Galapagos for seven years. What *he* had omitted to confess was that his stay had been involuntary—there was a convict settlement on the island of San Cristobal: Pedro Gonzalez had been one of the prisoners, but that didn't matter. What did matter was that their combined knowledge of navigation, and in fact common-sense seamanship was very scanty. Yet they were committed to finding the Galapagos, and when they got there to carrying out the task for which they had been sent. Their employer had wisely decreed that payment would be by results, he had provided *Black Jack* and enough stores to take her there and back. The reward would depend upon what they succeeded in acquiring.

He (their employer), was a sort of South American Barnum, a showman whose circuses travelled the length and breadth of the Continent with the usual collection of acrobats, clowns and caged beasts. Recently the gradual spread of television in the cities and travelling cinematograph shows in the country districts had caused a serious falling off of audiences, and Senor Pontivecchi was desperately anxious to acquire some novelties. Chancing one day to watch a travelogue film about the Galapagos he was struck with the idea of procuring a number of giant land turtles and iguanas

37

(a sort of prehistoric lizard) and the result of his sudden impulse was the setting forth of the *Black Jack* and her nondescript crew from the port of Buenaventura. The *Black Jack* had started life as a "Bluenose" schooner, used for cod-fishing on the Newfoundland Banks. At some time in her long life she had been converted to an auxiliary ketch, engined by a heavy-oil diesel which was far superior to her cut-down sail plan. Since Hooker and his mates knew little about sailing they had contented themselves with hoisting the mainsail and keeping the engine running. In so doing they made excellent progress, but when this story begins they had just discovered that they didn't know where they were. According to Hooker's reckoning the island of San Cristobal should be in sight. The weather was clear and the highest part of the island went up to two thousand feet. On such a day it should have been possible to have seen it over twenty miles away. According to Hooker it was far closer than that, but, strain their eyes though they did there was no land to be seen anywhere, and no tiny puffs of white cloud which so often betray the existence of land beneath the horizon.

To be lost at sea is a very worrying business, for having reached a position by calculation and found it to be incorrect the question then arises as to where to go next?

Many sailing vessels in the past have been obliged to give up the search of islands when their calculations have proved to be wrong. The humiliating experience of a Turkish man-of-war which failed to find the island of Malta has passed into legendary history. Years later, several ocean-racers on the New York-Bermuda run were unable to find their destination, and after several days' vain searching put back to the American continent which was impossible to miss.

Nowadays there are many more aids to navigation than

in the past. Celestial navigation (that is obtaining the ship's position by observation of stars, planets and the sun) has been simplified and the Time Signals sent round the world from Greenwich have guaranteed perfect accuracy in this all important science. All the observer has to do is to identify a heavenly body, and by means of a sextant to measure the angle between it and the horizon. Three objects taken at the same time will produce, by means of mathematical tables, three "position-times". Where these three lines meet on the chart is the ship's position. Simple enough—if you know how!

Then there are Radio Beacons which send out an easily recognisable "beam", the bearing (or angle) of which can be readily taken by means of the ship's compass and a directional aerial. In the placid seas and clear visibility which *Black Jack*'s crew had so far experienced there was no excuse for being lost. There were plenty of manuals and nautical tables aboard, there was a sextant, the compass looked business-like, there was an excellent patent-log for measuring the distance run; in fact there was everything except a trained navigator. Even so, *Black Jack* should have hit off an archipelago which stretched over an area nearly a hundred miles in diameter, and he probably would have if the remainder of the crew had obeyed their captain. Jeff Hooker was no fool, and had, before leaving harbour picked the brains of an old salt who had given him all instructions as to the course to steer and what allowance should be made for the very considerable ocean current which runs up to $2\frac{1}{2}$ knots. Unfortunately for the end result neither Pedro nor Cobbo, nor even Fatso, were in the right frame of mind to be careful about their steering, and in the night watches they usually lashed the wheel and had a quiet doze. So it wasn't surprising that they were lost. Jeff Hooker

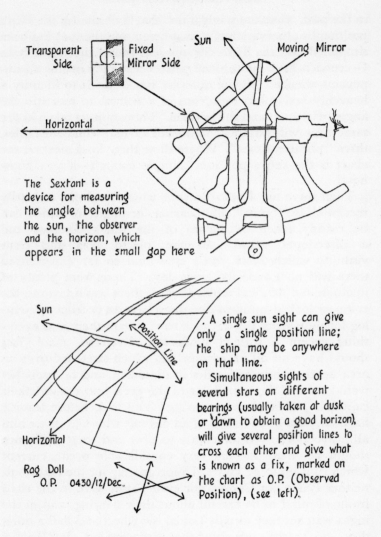

Transparent Side

Fixed Mirror Side

Sun

Moving Mirror

Horizontal

The Sextant is a device for measuring the angle between the sun, the observer and the horizon, which appears in the small gap here

Sun

Position Line

Horizontal

Rag Doll
O.P.   0430/12/Dec.

. A single sun sight can give only a single position line; the ship may be anywhere on that line.

Simultaneous sights of several stars on different bearings (usually taken at dusk or dawn to obtain a good horizon), will give several position lines to cross each other and give what is known as a fix, marked on the chart as O.P. (Observed Position), (see left).

40

had been in many more awkward situations than this. He'd
find the islands sooner or later, he said, and since he had no
idea in which direction to search he tossed a coin. "Heads
we go north, tails south!" he said. It came down heads and
course was altered due north. Luck had been good to them
for they were in fact forty miles south of the southernmost
island. Fortune usually favours the brave, but not the foolhardy; it was certainly foolhardy to have continued on their
course during the night when the visibility was down to a
few hundred yards.

At one in the morning Fatso heard the sound of breakers
dead ahead and called the Skipper. But too late. A few
moments later "*Black Jack*" struck a very nobby piece of
rock. Her bows rose sharply in the air and she fell over on
her side, a total wreck on the reef half a mile to the southward of Palmelo Island.

Chapter Five

TOM HUNTINGDON'S SECRET

TOM HUNTINGDON was always very careful to stick to the time-table he had made for himself when first he had settled down to his lonely existence on Palmelo Island. He knew almost by instinct that a solitary life, even when self-chosen could have a bad effect upon a man if he did not take a lot of trouble to maintain an outward semblance of civilised behaviour. Thus, he always rose at daylight, shaved and washed himself as carefully as if he was going to be inspected by an Admiral, cooked a proper breakfast, and ate it on a table laid with cloth, plate and cutlery, washed up, made the bed, turned on the radio, listened to the news, went to feed and water his animals, wrote up his daily diary, took his morning walk along the rocky fore-shore of the island, counted the various kinds of birds to be seen, looked for signs of nesting or moulting, and recorded everything in his notebook; watched the antics of the great sea-lions playing in the deeper water; amused himself pursuing the dignified little penguins; stepped deliberately over the dangerous "sea-eggs" whose prickles can poison a man's foot, and generally searched around for the daily harvest brought to the shore by the South Equatorial current.

As he pottered methodically his thoughts began to dwell on the visitors he was expecting. He had written the truth in his letter to Uncle George : his stay on the island had been of great benefit to him. He had had a difficult time after his release from the Japanese prisoner-of-war camp : his nerves had been in bad condition and he had begun to hate the sight of his fellow creatures, to shrink from the noises of the modern world and to abhor the smells of oil-refineries, petrol engines and smoke-laden fog which seemed to him to have increased in England beyond endurance during the past few years. Like so many war-weary people he had nourished a strong desire to "get away from it all" and when he had seen an advertisement which offered solitude and hard work in return for a fairly generous salary he had jumped at it.

He, like Senor Pontivecchi, had read and seen a good deal recently about the fabulous Galapagos, how they were a direct link with a long dead world, genuine uninhabited islands (that is by Man) until the all-conquering Spaniards had attempted to colonise them in the 17th Century, from their existing acquisitions on the west coast of South America. He had read too, how Charles Darwin in his famous ship the *Beagle* had found much that he was seeking on these islands, and how the great biologist had drawn from his observations there certain facts to support his theories on how life in the world had developed from its earliest stages. The Galapagos had virtually stood still in time for thousands of years, while the larger tracts of land though developing their own species had not always been populated by the same creatures. Changes in climate caused some animals to die out and others to seek fresh woods and pastures new. The strength and ferocity of some creatures caused the destruction of others—the whole pattern on the continents of the world was that of the "survival of the fittest", and on top of it all there was man, greedy for gain, hungry for food— man, who cut down the trees, planted vegetables, slaughtered some animals and bred others for domestic purposes, waged war, and destroyed his own edifices, dug in the ground for precious minerals, bedecked his women with the furs and feathers of wild creatures, killed the great monarchs of the sea in order to turn their blubber into oil for his lamps, grease for his bread and soap for his laundering. No living creature's life had been safe if his death would serve a purpose.

In all the pressure of the day-to-day struggle for existence which had gone on since the Spanish, Portuguese, Dutch, French and British pioneers had portioned out the New World between them no one had bothered much about the Galapagos. Only the great ships who roamed the ocean in search of whales had found them really useful. They used to put in for food, fruit and drinking water, and some mariners more far-sighted than others landed some cattle and goats who flourished on the high grounds and multiplied into great herds. Greatly prized were the giant land-turtles from which the islands drew their name, the Galapagos. These made excellent food for sailors whose usual diet consisted of salt pork and hard bread. The flesh of the turtle is a great delicacy and makes wonderful soup. With the coming of steam and the invention of refrigeration however, a visit to the Galapagos for food became unnecessary, and it was just as well that this was so, for the wild animals were disappearing too quickly and the rate of breeding young ones was insufficient to maintain replacements. If the Ecuadorian government had not stepped in and declared the whole Archipelago a Game Preserve Tom Huntingdon would have had little to observe. As it was there was plenty, both on land and in the seas around.

There was another factor which made the Galapagos unique. Although they were situated bang on the Equator, and ought to have been the hottest islands in the world, they were far from being so, and at night Tom would be glad of a couple of blankets over his bed. This was because a stream of cool water from the South Pacific Ocean washed the island shores reducing the temperature to something rather less than that of the Caribbean islands. And not only that— visitors from the polar regions had come to the islands regularly; many had taken up residence there thousands of years ago. They were the sea lions, the seals, the penguins—flightless cormorants, bosun-birds, frigate-birds, albatross, flamingos, owls and dozens of lesser known species which Tom Huntingdon photographed, catalogued and collected in egg-form as well as alive. The reptiles were no less fantastic, both in quantity and quality, and the waters teemed with every sort of fish. Insects, too were plentiful. Mosquitoes came out at night in solid clouds—hence the demand for D.D.T.—but the worst plague of all was one which man had brought along with the blessings of the cattle and goats. Rats! Thousands of them who preyed upon the young birds and anything else that was edible. Tom Huntingdon waged a steady war against those most unpleasant rodents, but did no more than hold his own. On a moonlit night they could be seen from the window of his shack, scurrying round in search of anything he had been careless enough to leave out. They were as fearless as the pigeons in Trafalgar Square and as difficult to catch.

Tom Huntingdon had taken it all in his stride. He'd known all about the disadvantages of the place before he had come, and nothing so far had surprised him beyond the discovery he had made almost immediately after taking up residence in the island. There was one sandy beach, facing north and sheltered from the prevailing south-easterly Trade Wind. A strong current from the South Equatorial Stream already described made bathing from it a hazardous affair, and Tom had once had a narrow escape from being swept away. At

45

the corner of the beach, however, was a little inlet, caused by the scouring effect of the current which curled round and ate away the shifting sands. There the water was safe for swimming; for the sharks did not come so close in, also Tom had been able to construct a short slipway by which he could winch up his motor-boat clear of the highest tides and safe from any storm which might have swept it away.

It was there also that Tom used to fish for his supper. The whole operation took a few minutes only, for he never took life for the pleasure of killing. A feather on a hook attached to a stout line, and thrown well out into the deep water would bring in a Tuna every time. No skill was required: it was handy to have a fishmongery just round the corner.

Tom soon discovered that practically any floating object would eventually fetch up on the beach of his little bay which he had for obvious reasons christened Tuna Cove. Among a collection of bottles, corks, grapefruit skins and the usual jetsam from ships which may well have passed a thousand miles south of the island Tom noticed some spongy whitish lumps which looked at first sight to be pumice-stones. He collected a few pieces for cleaning his fingers after painting, and then had found that they were not hard and porous like pumice, but soft and spongy with a curiously sweet aromatic smell.

He didn't have to be told what he'd found. He knew at once that here was ambergris, that most peculiar and valuable substance for which all who live near the sea in tropical zones are on the lookout. Ambergris, like another natural by-product, the pearl, which is formed by an oyster with "crumbs in its bed" is a sort of accidental deposit which gradually collects in the stomach of a sperm whale and more often than not eventually is discharged by the living animal. When this happens it floats in small lumps on the surface of

the sea and sooner or later it is washed up on island shores.
It begins its existence as a dull grey or blackish substance
with a disagreeable smell, but after it has been exposed to
sunlight it bleaches almost white and smells quite differently.
It is this peculiarly sweet and earthy odour that makes the
stuff so valuable to people who manufacture perfumes. An
ounce of ambergris is worth over three English pounds and
sometimes lumps weighing as much as one hundred pounds
(weight) have been found.

Tom Huntingdon realised at once that he was in the
position of a man who has won a football pool, or drawn a
prize for a Premium Bond, and as daily he added to his
collection he used to sing the most apposite of songs—
"Pennies from Heaven". The acquisition of this wealth,
however, brought its own especial problem—how to get it
away from the island unbeknown to the local officials. It
wasn't that he was not entitled to all the ambergris he could
find on the beach below the high-water mark, he was without a doubt being completely honest both legally and ethically
in regarding the stuff as his property, but he knew that he
was alone and without friends, and he knew enough about
the ways and morals of some of the local officials to be aware
that if once his valuable collection were discovered he could
say good-bye to it, for that which would not be actually
stolen would be subjected to enormous Excise Duties when
he landed it on South American soil. And, since he would
not have the money to pay these duties, his entire stock of the
treasure would probably be confiscated. It was an exasperating situation for poor Tom. Almost every day his
collection of ambergris increased: it was like being the owner
of a taxi-cab, watching the meter ticking up the sixpences
hour by hour and wondering whether the man inside could
pay! Week after week he became richer and richer, and his

hoard had increased in volume until he could no longer keep it in his shack; so he had stowed it in empty oil cans which he stocked in a small cave some hundred yards away. The thought of this valuable hoard was always with him and because he spent twenty-nine days out of every thirty entirely alone he was beginning to become obsessed by his secret, just as misers keep counting their money, half gloating over its possession and half afraid of robbers and thieves.

The thirtieth day, when he was not alone, was spent on the adjacent island of San Cristobal the official "capital" of the Archipelago and headquarters of the local government. It was there that he obtained his staple foods: flour, beans, coffee, sugar, meat etc; these were brought to the island by the regular boat for Guayaquil which also handled the mails. His monthly trip by motor-boat to San Cristobal was not entirely pleasant, for he was a foreigner, performing his duties under licence of the Ecuadorian Government, and he was obliged to report himself to the Chief of Police— Colonel Gaspardo—a pleasant enough gentleman, but a very inquisitive-minded one, who having long since discovered all there was to know about every other inhabitant of his own island found the occasions of Tom's visit a welcome break in the monotony of his existence. During the past four years of his tenure of office as Chief of Police there had been little crime on any of the islands, no violence and no poaching of the natural game. Poor Colonel Gaspardo was bored stiff. It would have suited him better if Tom's background had been shrouded in mystery, but this was not so. The Christopherson Research Foundation had furnished every possible item of information about their appointed agent, whose character was clearly beyond reproach. Notwithstanding this, however, the Colonel was careful to open and read every letter which arrived for Tom from abroad and did the same to all outgoing ones that Tom had written. Of this Tom was aware. Whether the Colonel knew that Tom knew was difficult to say. It was a pleasant game for the Colonel, pretending to himself that Tom was a dangerous spy. If it had not been for the existence of the ambergris his 'cat and mouse' act wouldn't have mattered at all : as it was it tied Tom's hands completely. He was a virtual prisoner during his sojourn in Palmelo : he could not communicate with the outside world in privacy. It can be readily imagined how welcome was the news of the impending visit of *Rag Doll*. Here was the answer to all his problems.

Chapter Six

A VISIT TO SAN CRISTOBAL

O N the morning of December the twentieth Tom Huntingdon was up earlier than usual, for this was to be the
day on which he was to pay his monthly visit to San Cristobal. He had not slept very well because the weather during
the previous day had been a worry. A thick driving mist had
reduced the visibility to a few hundred yards, making the
twenty-miles voyage to San Cristobal far too hazardous to be
undertaken.

His first action, therefore, on waking to the first notes of his
alarm clock was to go quickly out on to his verandah to see
what sort of day it was. With great relief he saw that the
mist had disappeared, the wind had dropped and everything
looked favourable for the considerable journey he was about
to undertake.

Before leaving he went about his preparations with great
care. Accidents and breakdowns were always possible and
since he was expecting the arrival of *Rag Doll* at any
moment he made sure that Uncle George would be aware of
the situation by leaving a note pinned to the living-room
table. Then he climbed to the highest point of the island
and stood there waiting for the sunrise, his telescope in hand.
This was a daily action and one which he always undertook
with a feeling of eager anticipation akin to that of a house-
holder when he goes to his door after hearing the postman's
knock. What would the day bring forth? Twice during his
lonely sojourn he had sighted the sails of a small boat and had

hoped that the voyagers would put in at Palmelo, and twice he had been disappointed. This time, if a sail was in sight it would be almost certainly that of *Rag Doll* and he would defer his trip to San Cristobal.

As he climbed the little track to the summit the place seemed to quiver and shake with life. Small animals moved quickly into hiding, wild goats pretended to be frightened of him, more for the sake of a new sensation than from any real fear. Lizards and snakes darted across the path, and, as the first pink rays of the sun shone in the massive craggy surfaces of the rocky hill-top a great cloud of owls rose in the air and filled it with the sound of a thousand fluttering wings. After the rain the place smelt sweet and Tom felt his spirits rising. He gained the summit and waited for the sun to emerge completely from the eastern horizon. It would be no good trying to look for a sail in that direction while that great blazing orb was on the level of the ocean. While he waited he turned and searched all other points of the compass. Away to the west some five miles distant was the craggy island named "Little Palmelo", uninhabited save by sea lions, lizards and turtles. Further away still he could see Santa Fé and beyond it, wreathed in early morning mist the twin peaks of Santa Cruz. Down below the sea fretted on the shore, making a continuous roar which was penetrated by the mournful barking of lonely sea lions calling for their mates. In the shallow lake half-way down the hill a great flock of flamingo stood motionless waiting for the day to begin. It was all very much the same as usual.

Down to the southward he could just see the grey outline of San Cristobal. The sea looked calm enough, which was reassuring, for the motor-boat was not very large and some-times the south-east Trade Wind would pipe up to strong, making the journey a wet and difficult one. Today he felt all

51

would be well, though such light winds would be unlikely to bring *Rag Doll* along. Nevertheless he turned once more to the eastward and searched the horizon with great care, using a coloured glass shade for his telescope. There was nothing to be seen except the beautiful deep-blue texture of the sea and the great golden avenue of the sun's rays. Such a morning as this, he reflected made life worth living—"every prospect pleases" he quoted and then wished he had not, for he remembered the line which followed:—"and only man is vile". As if in answer to his thoughts he heard a man's voice raised in anger—at least he thought he heard it—and so did the flock of flamingos which rose like a pink and white cloud and flew around aimlessly before settling again on the mirror-like waters of their little lake. Then a great honking and roaring from down on the rocks beneath him sent the birds aloft again. Two sea lions fighting, that was all. He took another look round and then went down to his shack to prepare for the journey.

Half an hour later he was ready to go. He loaded the motor-boat with empty crates and a good supply of drinking water in case of accidents, and taking the brake off the winch allowed the boat to slip silently into the little cove. Jumping aboard he unhooked the tackle, wound up the engine and backed cautiously out into deep water, before setting out to round the island and so to get on his course to San Cristobal. Now the sun was well up—the day was perfect for the crossing. He reached the easternmost point of Palmelo and swung the bows until the compass course was dead south. Twenty miles to go: in these conditions he would be at Bahia Wreck (Wreck Bay) in time for breakfast with Colonel Gaspardo. All was well in the best of all possible worlds. He lifted up his voice and sang "Pennies from Heaven". It never occurred to him to look astern at the weather side of the island where the swell was breaking on the outlaying reef. If he had he might have seen the tip of a mast just before it disintegrated in the boiling surf, and ashore the last remaining wreaths of a wood fire which was being stamped out before its presence betrayed the existence of men—four men—four vile men.

Chapter Seven

FOUR VILE MEN!

"STOP that, Fatso, d'you hear!"

Jeff Hooker raised a great fist meaningly. Fatso Arbuckle who had started to wave his off-white shirt, dropped it obediently.

"So why?" he protested. "That's a motor-boat with a man in it! Seems the island is inhabited."

"No," said Pedro Gonzalez, "not. Dis island game preservative only. 'Tis true. Yes!"

"Then what's that guy doing around here?" asked Cobbo.

"Maybe he's a game-warden", said Jeff Hooker. "If he is he'll be back in a day or two, or maybe a week."

"Why did you not let me flag him?" went on Fatso indignantly. "We gotta get off this island, haven't we?"

Jeff Hooker scratched his stubbly chin. "Look!" he said earnestly. "We've had a bit o' bad. I'm not blaming anyone, though I could if I wanted to. This is no time for recrimination. We're shipwrecked. We've touched bottom."

"You're telling me," added Fatso.

"Shipwrecked mariners don't get treated so good in these parts, eh Pedro?" asked Jeff Hooker.

"Dat is so. Maybe dey lock us all up 'longside de convicts. Not nice folks belong here", said Pedro.

"That's how I figured", said Jeff. "There's no sense in giving ourselves up while there's a chance of doing better, is there?"

The four vile man were squatting in the rocky foreshore, watching Tom Huntingdon's motor-boat speeding away. Their dinghy lay where the surf had thrown it; its contents had been salved and were laid out to dry in the morning sunshine. They were a revolver, a box of ammunition, oars, a bag of hard bread, a few tins of bully-beef, and a bottle of rum, all that they had had time to snatch up before *Black Jack* had foundered.

Close behind them a great bull sea lion raised itself on its tail and clapped its flappers as it roared its defiance of the invaders.

"Aw! Go an' chase yourself!" said Fatso. He picked up a stone and hurled it at the brute which retreated a few feet while continuing to roar lustily. "For cryin' out loud!" went on the exasperated Fatso. He bent down and picked up something else. "Put a sock in it! Can't you!"

"Just a minute!" Jeff Hooker's hand shot out to grab hold of Fatso's as he prepared to throw.

"Now what is it?" said Fatso, "maybe you belong to the League of Pity, or somep'n? If I want to heave a brick at yonder so-and-so where's the harm in it?"

Jeff Hooker's powerful fingers prised open Fatso's hand. "Take it easy, Fatso," he said. "Just let me have a load of this." He picked the missile out of the American's palm and put it to his nose. As he took a sniff at it his eyes lit up. Then he slipped the lump into his trouser pocket. "You don't want to go throwing good money about", he said, "this here's valuable. Ambergris."

"Whoopee!" Fatso leapt to his feet and removing his battered straw-hat bowed to the sea lion. "Thanks pal!" he said.

Without a further word the four men began to move along the foreshore, searching the spaces between the rocks for

55

more ambergris. In this they were successful and soon each one of them had found a bit.

"See what I mean", said Jeff Hooker, as they foregathered again. "We've found a little gold-mine—and we don't want to be in too much of a hurry to leave it."

"What's the good of us collecting it?" asked Cobbo—"the ruddy dagos will have it all off us as quick as kiss-yer-hand."

Jeff Hooker nodded. "This wants thinking out," he said. "Between us in about an hour we've collected about twenty quid's worth. Supposing we spent a few weeks here and stacked all our findings somewhere safe. Then when we're rescued we'll say nothing about it. Then, maybe we can come back and fetch it when nobody's looking."

There was a silence as each member mentally registered his intention of being the first to return (and alone) for the boodle.

Cobbo spoke next. "How come you do all the talking, Jeff?" he said. "You *was* the skipper—but you ain't now. We're all equal, I reckon."

"Not entirely," said Jeff Hooker, as his hand strayed to the revolver which had unobtrusively found its way to his belt. "Not entirely. You treat me fair and I do likewise. I brought you here to this place and maybe I'll get you off again richer than when you came; but no funny business."

To ram home the significance of his speech he pulled out his pistol and fired it in the general direction of the old sea lion. The noise of the shot roused every bird on the beach; great clouds of boobies, gulls, albatross, parrots and owls screamed aloft as if in witness to Jeff Hooker's pronouncement. When the clamour had died Pedro Gonzales was the next to speak.

"Dis man is alright", he said. "He belong our Captain—I belong him."

Cobbo and Fatso eyed each other and then grinned. "O.K." said Fatso. "We're your slaves, Mister. Where do we go from here?"

Jeff Hooker replaced his revolver. "First things first," he said, "get the dinghy afloat and go out and salve all you can from *Black Jack*. After that we'll explore the island and set up a camp."

After some difficulty the dinghy was refloated, Pedro took the oars while the other two stripped off ready to slip over the side when the position of the wreck was reached. Fatso, sitting in a warm pair of pants looked like an overgrown boy; Cobbo, on the other hand was as lean and scraggy as a scarecrow. Neither of them relished the idea of getting wet and both were a bit scared of the unknown. Jeff Hooker seated himself in a commanding position ashore and lit his pipe. There was a good deal of thinking to be done, he reckoned, and that sort of thinking needed solitude.

"Say!" said Fatso, shivering slightly, though the air was warm and caressing. "Do they keep sharks in these parts, Pedro?"

"Sure, plenty sharks", said Pedro happily. "They come, I tell you. Not to worry."

"Thank you for nothing", said Cobbo, and eyed his companion with satisfaction. "If they do fancy a bite at us, Fatso, I reckon as how you'd be the one they'd go for. All that blubber—you could spare a bit of it easy, couldn't he, Pedro?"

Pedro showed his teeth. "You be all right," he said, "sharks not come in so close on account of the Iguanas."

"How much? What's them?" Fatso looked nervously round him. Pedro shook his head. "Not to worry", he repeated and drew up alongside *Black Jack*'s topmast which projected some few feet above the surface. The water was as clear as crystal and the whole of the wrecked vessel could be seen lying on her side below the dinghy. As they stared through the wavy surface of the sea they saw a shoal of brightly-coloured fish swimming languidly out of the open hatch.

"They haven't taken long to move in", said Cobbo. He grasped the mast, took a deep breath and hoisted himself overboard. Fatso watched him pulling himself down to the deck by means of the halliards, but made no attempt to follow.

"You not go?" asked Pedro.

"Maybe he'll need help," said Fatso. "I'll just stand by in case."

Cobbo had by now disappeared into the saloon. He was out of sight for about a quarter of a minute only, then he shot into view, kicking desperately, and came quickly to the surface. As he did so a great lizard-like creature also emerged from the vessel's interior and swam swiftly towards the shore. It was over a yard long and looked so ferocious, with its spiked backbone and knobby excrescences, that no one should have blamed Cobbo for his panic.

"Help, help!" he gasped.

Pedro burst out laughing. "Ha ha ha! Not to worry! Dat's Iguana. Not eat man, not eat fish; only vegetables. Very stupid animals, not to worry."

"All right", said Cobbo. "If that's so, how about you going down, hey?"

"No can swim", said Pedro firmly.

"How about you?" Cobbo turned to Fatso.

"I can't sink on account I'm so fat", said the American. "Mighty sorry, but that's how it is!" His steady little eyes showed his determination to keep out of water at all costs.

"Yellow!" spat Cobbo, and to prove that he was made of

No one should have blamed Cobbo for his panic.

sterner stuff went down again. This time he remained down long enough to find an iron bucket and a bit of line, one end of which he tied to the handle and the other he brought up to Fatso. Then he went down again and began to load the bucket with tinned foods—the lighter stuff he allowed to float to the surface.

Presently the dinghy was loaded to the gunwhale and returned to the shore where Jeff was waiting. He had seen all that was going on and registered the thought that of the three men he could rule out Fatso as a danger to the plans which were forming in his mind. Cobbo he could see was a different proposition, and Pedro had in a drunken fit confided that his seven years' imprisonment had been the result of a fracas with a knife. "I jus' cut a little piece of t'roat. Silly man he jus' lay down and die. Too bad, not to worry." Pedro would have to be watched.

All the morning Cobbo worked like a beaver until the contents of *Black Jack*'s capacious lockers had been brought ashore. For his efforts Jeff awarded him a hearty swig from the rum bottle. Then a tin of bully-beef and a box of hard bread were broached and the four men made a hearty meal.

After they'd filled their stomachs all four stretched out on the warm shingle and relaxed. Soon a trio of snores in muddled close-harmony told its own tale. Jeff waited for a while, and then rising quickly he tiptoed away on a voyage of exploration.

It didn't take him long to find one of the various worn paths made by Tom Huntingdon on his daily rounds. By following it he came upon the shack and after a loud "Hello there!" he entered it and looked around him.

Everything he saw pointed to the fact that only one man was living there. A single-bed neatly made, two plates, a knife and fork, even a table napkin, all gave evidence, not only of the existence of a solitary occupant but of his character. Here was no beach-comber. No stack of empty liquor bottles; the floor had been swept recently—the mosquito-nets were freshly laundered, the place smelt clean and was pleasantly cool.

Jeff looked round him with increasing interest. In the corner of the room was a desk whose drawers were full of papers. On the wall were several shelves lined with books. Half a dozen parakeets twittered on the cross-beams which supported the roof. They were not alarmed by his presence. Jeff examined a few papers and a daily journal, casually at first and then with increasing interest. Moving into the alcove which the presence of a paraffin-stove suggested as being the kitchen he found a piece of paper pinned to the small deal table.

"Commander Firebrace," it ran, "in case you arrive before I get back this is to bid you welcome. There's good holding-ground just off the boat-slip and you'll be more comfortable afloat than on this mosquito-ridden island." Signed "Tom".

Tom. Commander Firebrace. Tom's journals. Firebrace's letter. Tom's meticulous habit of filing carbon-copies of all his letters. The situation pieced itself together as easily as a child's jigsaw puzzle. And, to make things even more attractive were the references to the collection of ambergris. Tom Huntingdon had kept a separate tally of the stuff he'd collected, the total of which made Jeff Hooker's hair curl. It took no time at all to find the cave and to examine the fuel-drums. A small fortune lay there for the taking. It was just a question of how to arrange matters. Another occasion for doing some deep thinking. It was a pity that the three others were safely ashore. Something would have to be done about them and about Mister Tom Huntingdon, not to mention this chap Commander Firebrace and his crew. It all looked very promising but first to do some thinking. After a while Jeff took a piece of paper and inserting it into Tom's typewriter began to type. It was going *to be quite simple*!

Chapter Eight

"RAG DOLL" ON PASSAGE

"NO wonder they call this the Pacific Ocean", said Loopy as he lolled under the cockpit awning and listened drowsily to the beat of *Rag Doll*'s diesel. "Four days out and not a breath of wind. How's the fuel-supply working out, Commander?"

Uncle George knocked his pipe out on the gunwale before replying. "I can spare enough for another twenty-four hours' running," he said: "after that we must conserve what we have left and wait for the wind."

Ever since leaving Balboa *Rag Doll* had ploughed her way on a southerly course in breathless humid weather, searching for a breeze. Conditions in the vicinity of the Gulf of Panama are notoriously bad for sailing vessels and the ocean-currents behave in an exasperating manner, circling the Gulf so that a vessel becalmed will be carried nowhere in particular. Many an engineless vessel in the past had been caught in this slow-moving whirlpool in baffling airs insufficient to move any but the swiftest of ships, while all the time the hull would gather more and more marine growths, so that when the wind eventually did come the ship's bottom would be so festooned with weeds that she would be unable to move fast enough to combat the current. Thanks to Uncle George's foresight in loading up with extra fuel those aboard *Rag Doll* had been spared the slow torture of hundreds of hours of flat calms. "Aunt Bertha", as they called the diesel engine—(Loopy said he had an aunt who made a similar noise when she was eating: no one believed him, but the name had stuck)—Aunt Bertha was chugging along in a very satisfactory manner. Away to port they had an occasional glimpse of the snow-capped peaks of the mighty Andes, sometimes as far distant as sixty miles. Now the equator was not far off, yet because of the cooling current the water temperature was not unduly high and the awnings which covered *Rag Doll* combined with the breeze made by her as she clocked up her seven to eight knots kept conditions almost ideally warm. No one was wearing more than the barest minimum of clothing and occasionally they would all gather on deck for a good hosing down from the engine-operated pump. After that there would be water-fights with canvas buckets, the combatants scooping up the crystal-clear ocean. Many longing glances had been cast upon this beautiful sea which looked so inviting and beckoned the unwary to slip into its cool embrace, but Uncle George had given the strictest orders that not even a toe was to be dipped into it. To illustrate his reason for such an edict he had tossed a ham-bone overboard. There was little enough meat left on the joint but what there was was sufficient to attract the immediate attention of several fish. Within a few seconds the sea had come alive with sharks of all sizes, ranging from one monster over twelve feet long to some of half that size. They snapped at the sinking bone, twisting and turning as they did so. It was an impressive display, and no one suggested a swim after that. At night sometimes, they would feel *Rag Doll* moving in an unnatural way and could hear a rasping sound under her keel. Sharks were rubbing themselves free of irritating parasites while they escorted the vessel, patiently waiting for a special meal until hunger would drive them off in search of a more easily obtainable but less attractive feast of small fishes. The thought of this ocean which teemed with life was always with them and though sometimes they dreamed of the menaces under the water there were plenty of compensations in watching their antics. Only those who sail in small boats can have any idea of the extent of marine life all around them. Passengers in great ocean liners may be lucky enough occasionally to see a school of whales or a basking shark, as well as the usual run of flying-fish, but in a vessel the size of *Rag Doll* one becomes a part of the marine life, and sometimes uncomfortably so.

One evening when Ted Tottle was endeavouring to improve the minds of the Green Sailors by reading extracts from the classics, Uncle George let out a stentorian yell and brought them up on deck to see a most extraordinary sight. A giant sting-ray—looking like a great black bat and half as wide as *Rag Doll* was long was jumping clean out of the sea, falling back in a series of mighty slaps which sent columns of

A giant sting ray . . . was jumping clear out of the sea.

green water almost mast-high. It was an awe-inspiring sight to see such energy, for the fish must have weighed several tons, and all this, explained Uncle George, was to rid itself of the small parasites which had taken up residence on its body and were driving it frantic with irritation. It was fortunate, he said, that that particular type of fish hadn't the wit to scratch its back like the sharks did. It was difficult after that exhibition to return to the placid works of Jane Austen.

Ted Tottle was certainly having his work cut out in keeping his side of the bargain with the Green parents. It was all very fine to decide to settle down to an educational curriculm, but the trouble was that with all the will in the world it was impossible to prevent the surrounding natural phenomena from taking one's mind off the work.

In an attempt to make 'school' more palatable Ted, in an arithmetic lesson took a problem which said: 'Four men working five hours a day can mow a field of grass in five days; how many men working at twice that rate could mow a field half as big?' and substituted sharks for men and mackerel for the hay-field. It had certainly stimulated the interest of Binnie and Ben who talked natural-history at full speed, but far from the arithmetic getting along faster it had resulted only in an argument as to whether blue sharks ate mackerel. "Do cats eat bats?" Ted didn't repeat that error.

Mark was better off than the others, in that his arithmetic was useful; he had taken on the job of working out Uncle George's "sights", (as his astronomical observations with a sextant were called), and soon became quite expert in the use of the various books of tables which are necessary in these calculations. It was almost exciting to work out long formulae and to see the results at the end transferred on to the chart so that one could say—"we're there!"

Mary, too, was better off in that her main studies were of English literature. That, in common parlance, meant "curling up with a good book" and who minds that on a warm day? No, poor Binnie and Ben were the sufferers, not to mention the chap who was trying to teach them, and Uncle George didn't make things any easier by calling them up to see something or other, pretty nearly all the time.

There was so much to see, and all in "beautiful technicolour". Rainbow-hued kingfish, dolphins, albacores, golden-spotted mackerel, tuna and wahoo lived and died excitingly as they were hunted by each other and the sharks. Hardly a moment passed without evidence of the external struggle for survival which was taking place. In the air, so close to the South American continent *Rag Doll* was followed by a great assortment of birds ranging in size from beautiful little coloured swallows to the hungry boobies and even fiercer men-of-war birds. It was a source of continual wonder that life could continue in such profusion when everything ate everything else, and nobody seemed to eat the sharks. Twice during one day *Rag Doll* was obliged to make a rapid alteration of course to avoid collision with a huge whale and once in the middle of the night she came to a sudden halt as the result of having hit one of those under-water monsters. It was all pretty breath-taking and not conducive to earnest study, but Ted stuck to the job and saw to it that the stipulated hours of work were adhered to, if only in the letter rather than the spirit of the bargain made with the Green parents.

Uncle George, looking happier and younger than they'd ever seen him, was revelling in these new experiences. He had never before been in that part of the world and found it fully up to the descriptions he had read in many books. He was very pleased with the way his nephews and nieces were shaping and grateful to Ted for trying so hard to keep them instructed; but he didn't worry as to how much they were learning—from books. There were more important things than that: self-reliance, ability to live at close-quarters with one's shipmates, the recognition of what constituted real danger, instant obedience when the occasion demanded it, and the liveliest of interests in everything that was going on. These would be of far greater value to the Greens in later life than the Fifth Proposition of Euclid but he warned them that when the cruise was over they would have to do some intensive swotting to reach the standard of those who had not been so lucky as they. And being proper people the Greens took no notice of the warnings. Tomorrow was another day—in the meantime here they were, half-way to the most extraordinary islands in the world, in perfect weather and in their dearly loved *Rag Doll* which had so far brought them safely through so many adventures.

Only Loopy was a bit restless. He was half regretting his decision to continue the voyage, instead of seeking a new environment. Life for four whole days had been too settled; this schooling and natural history was all very well—the sea was blue and the fishes were beautiful, but Oh Gee! he'd never been fond of aquariums, and how he disliked the sound of Aunt Bertha! He whistled tunelessly and stuck his knife in the mast: both were supposed to be proved methods of conjuring up the spirit of the winds, but nothing happened. Tomorrow he knew that Uncle George was going to turn off the engine and after that they would be at the mercy of the currents. He'd read of a sailing ship which had been caught in a calm for thirty whole days until having run out of water and provisions the crew had abandoned ship and rowed ashore. A nice thought that!

He stretched himself and went into the deck-house where Mark was plotting the result of his latest calculations.

"Gee!" said Loopy, "only forty miles north of the Equator—I've never 'crossed the line', have you?"

Uncle George's eyes twinkled as he heard him. Of course! There must be a crossing-the-line ceremony; that would occupy their minds as they drifted, waiting for the wind, which could not long be delayed. Accordingly he called to Loopy and together they hatched a plot.

That evening, just after supper Aunt Bertha suddenly stopped. The Greens were all down below, having been ordered rather mysteriously to get cracking with the washing-up. Uncle George muttering about having a wash and a shave had departed to the toilet to disguise himself. Ted and Loopy were in the cockpit.

The sudden cessation of the rhythmical beat of the engine left a sort of vacuum of noise. Voices which had been raised to overtop the pitch of Aunt Bertha's endless chewing now sounded far too loud.

"That's torn it!" said Loopy. "Somep'n's gone wrong with the motor."

"Shall I have a look at it?" asked Ted who had not been included in the plot.

"Hold it!" said Loopy—"Hark! D'you hear somep'n?"

Ted strained his ears, and so did the Greens in the saloon.

"What is it?" called Mary.

"Somep'n on the bowsprit. Come up everybody!"

They came quickly into the darkness of the velvet night and peered anxiously around them.

"There!" cried Loopy dramatically.

At that moment a sepulchral voice called.

"Ship ahoy! Ship ahoy!" It was curiously distorted and

in the sudden silence created by the stopping of the engine it sounded almost ghostly.

"Who's there?" called Loopy.

"King Neptune", came the voice. "You are entering my domain. Who are you?"

"We are faithful subjects of Your Majesty, King Neptune. Will you come aboard, sir?"

By this time the Greens had recovered from their first surprise and were beginning to recognise the voice, but when Loopy suddenly switched on the searchlight and shone it on the bowsprit they let out involuntary gasps. Perched on the far end was a bearded man with long hair on which was planted a glittering crown. In one hand he carried a Trident: his costume shone like the scales of a fish and his eyes gleamed in the garish light.

"Hail to you!" said Father Neptune; he crawled cautiously along the bowsprit until he had reached the deck. Then he rose to his full height and came aft.

"All who have never before crossed my line must be shaved," boomed Father Neptune.

Loopy went below and returned with a bowl of froth, a very large brush and a great wooden "razor" which he had fashioned from a spare sail-batten. Before he had time to escape Mark was seized by Father Neptune at the scruff of his neck and Loopy prodded him in the tummy so that he opened his mouth in time to get a brushful of soap in it. "Help!" he cried.

The Greens closed upon Father Neptune and the fight became general. Shaving soap flew in all directions and Ted seizing his opportunity restarted the engine so that the salt-water pump began to deliver a great stream which drenched Father Neptune and all around him. The struggle was fast and furious, for the Greens had been momentarily scared and were determined to get their own back on Uncle George who by now had been stripped of his false whiskers. It was glorious fun, and after they had chased him out of the cockpit they turned on Loopy, his accomplice, and well and truly "shaved" him, filling his mouth with froth until he finished them off by blowing bubbles so that they became helpless with laughter and had to let him go.

Then, as they towelled themselves down before going below, each to receive a "Crossing the line Certificate", a new sensation was felt. A cool breeze was blowing from astern.

"That's it!" shouted Uncle George. "The wind's come at last!"

Up went the sails. Aunt Bertha subsided into silence. *Rag Doll* began to heel and a satisfactory fizzing sound came from her fore-foot.

Loopy, standing up on the deck, adjusted the sheets to the freshening breeze which was coming from the south-east.

"Thanks, Neptune!" he called.

Away astern a big fish jumped, as if in acknowledgement.

"Course, due West!" called Uncle George. "Galapagos, here we come!"

Chapter Nine

BREAKFAST WITH COLONEL GASPARDO
AND HOME FOR SUPPER

AN evening squall was brewing as Tom Huntingdon set out from Wreck Bay on his return journey. A dark cloud lay ahead of him; it towered skywards as if it were the product of a man-made explosion, but jagged forks of lightning proclaimed its natural origin. These evening storms were common enough and greatly liked by the hard-working islanders who relied on them for a little extra water beyond the moist clouds which supplied the high lands, but not the low-lying districts. A heavy downpour was always welcome to people whose lives depended upon their crops, but not to a lone man in a small open boat, loaded with a mixture of perishable articles and tinned foods. With a philosophical shrug of his shoulders, however, Tom notched the throttle-lever to full speed, lit his pipe and settled down to steer the boat on its most advantageous course for com-bating the current. He knew these storms of old and was glad that he had declined Colonel Gaspardo's pressing in-vitation to stay for luncheon.

The Colonel had been in a most benevolent mood and had royally entertained his visitor with a breakfast of hot newly-baked bread, excellent coffee and a fish kedgeree, the nature of whose contents it would have been unwise to have inquired. Tom had long since schooled himself to swallow anything and everything that was put in front of him, and if the thought did occur to him that he was probably con-

72

suming slugs, snails, creatures of the insect world and octo-
puses he let it pass and thankfully downed the half-tumbler
of Spanish brandy which as an ex-medical man he assured
himself was an excellent antidote for almost anything he
had already swallowed.

His arrival at Wreck Bay had been reported in time for the
Colonel to send down a posse of his troops with a spare horse
which he had willingly mounted, for the journey to Progresso,
the situation of Police Headquarters, was five miles uphill
along dusty rutted roads, and it was not until the last
half-mile was reached that the scenery had become lush and
tropical with groves of oranges and olives to remind him of
less exotic places.

It had been an amusing day, for the Colonel, having
opened and read all Tom's correspondence was in a fever to
know about the projected visit of *Rag Doll*, and Tom was
equally determined to make the Colonel admit that he had
already obtained such information as did exist.

The game had consisted of Tom making some sort of reference to something in the correspondence: Christmas for
example. The Colonel had sniffed at the bait and nibbled a
little at it.

"My poor fellow," he ventured: "to be all alone at this
festival of the family. Do you not miss your friends?" To
which Tom had replied: "I shall not be alone," and then,
after a long pause he had added: "There are so many
creatures on the island that I am never alone."

After a mouthful or two more of the kedgeree Tom had
started another hare. "You have not paid Palmelo Island an
official visit for some months, Colonel. You will be coming
again soon?"

A cunning look came into the Colonel's eyes.

"Maybe yes, maybe no. A solitary man on Palmelo

cannot be suspected of law-breaking—is that not so? Why do you wish me to pay you a call?"

Tom grinned. "If I knew when you were coming—I would be able to"—he paused again—"make my arrangements. How is crime these days, Colonel?"

The Colonel frowned.

"Crime is never a joke, Senor. The law must always be observed for the protection of the innocent and the apprehension of the guilty. For example"—he spoke as carelessly as he could manage—"it may be a small thing in the eyes of a foreigner that the laws of my country insist that visitors to these islands will first report to me, the Chief of Police here, but any failure to do so might have serious consequences."

"My dear Colonel," Tom Huntingdon smiled blandly, "who would not wish to pay his compliments to so charming a host?"

"And in departing also, remember that!" The Colonel lit a black cheroot whose pungency even the mosquitoes respected.

"I speak to you, Senor, because I have Intelligence from Headquarters in my country that certain parties"—he coughed meaningly—"ostensibly on pleasure-bent may be on their way to these islands to—to poach—that is the correct word?"

"I was about to congratulate you on your remarkable grasp of my language, Colonel. It is strange to find such a gifted linguist as yourself languishing—if I may so express myself—in this faraway place."

"Let me advise you, Senor," said the Colonel, "never to learn a foreign language as well as I have learned English, or you too may find yourself in a similar position as I am. The only 'adventurers' who visit these islands are English-speaking and because of this I am sent here to interrogate them."

74

"And how many of these visitors have you so far interrogated?"

The Colonel looked sad.

"The spirit of adventure is not what it was," he observed, "it is four years since my knowledge of your language was usefully employed."

"Perhaps," said Tom blandly, "perhaps even now there may be people on the way and you will at long last be able to exercise your undoubted abilities. The Christmas period is a likely one for long-distance sailors."

"Of that I am aware", said Colonel Gaspardo. "I have radioed Headquarters for a Patrol Boat. And if I find any vessel in these waters which has not cleared itself at San Cristobal there will be much trouble. If any should come to you you will send them immediately—will you not?"

"Assuredly, Colonel", said Tom as he departed. "You may count on me to observe the laws of your country."

When he had gone the Colonel took out copies of the letters which had passed between Uncle George and Tom. He twisted his starboard moustachio as he re-read the two missives.

"The cunning fox," he said, "he thinks to pull wool over my eyes, but I am too old a wheat to be caught with such chaff!" He was aware that his metaphors were a trifle mixed but their meaning was plain enough. And, of course, it was Tom's own fault for not telling Gaspardo about *Rag Doll*. Tom's point of view was that the Colonel already knew the truth by committing the unpardonable sin of cribbing private correspondence. It served him right therefore if he had been led to suspect *Rag Doll* of nefarious intentions. Besides there was the little matter of the ambergris!

. . .

When only a few miles from Palmelo Tom saw the rain hanging over the island like a black curtain and felt the first cool draughts which whipped the sea into angry wavelets. The sun was sinking fast by now, for progress had been slow in the spring tides which seemed to be running with greater strengths than he had ever known. To add to the general unsatisfactoriness of his situation the engine had begun to labour as the result of having been run overlong at full throttle and he was obliged to switch it off for a spell to allow it to cool. Being a man of resource he did not sit and twiddle his thumbs; instead he erected a sail by means of his two oars and an oilskin. One oar was threaded through both sleeves as in the manner of a scarecrow and the other was lashed at right angles to the first to form a cross. Two lengths of twine fixed to the corners of the oilskin "skirts" acted as "sheets" and the sail was then ready for hoisting,

which meant that Tom had to "step" it amongst his cargo and to hold the sheets against the pressure of the following wind.

In this manner a boat kept moving *through* the water,

though making little progress *over* the land. It was going to be a dark night and Tom had left no guiding light to help him find Tuna Cove; as time wore on therefore he began to feel a trifle anxious. He schooled his impatience however, as long as he dared, so that the engine which was still fizzling as the raindrops touched it, could cool further. With the sun disappearing suddenly behind the rather ominous bank of clouds over Little Palmelo he decided to get going again. Down came the sail and off went the engine.

Reaching the end of the island Tom steered under its lee and safely navigated into Tuna Cove while the rain came down like silver rods, adding considerably to the weight of the boat.

It was a real struggle, winching her up the slipway, but he managed to get her up far enough to move the plug from her bilges and so to drain the heavy load of water in them. Once that had been done he was able to wind the boat right up and then he set about unloading the provisions on to a rough wooden sledge that he had previously knocked together and which he was able to drag along the track leading to his home. By the time he'd piled all the gear on the sledge and covered it with a piece of canvas the sun had set and the rain, having done its worst stopped as suddenly as it had begun. Immediately the air was filled with a wonderful odour and the night chorus of crickets and frogs emerged above the sound of cascading water. Little torrents were splashing down the track, lubricating the "runners" of the sledge and making it easier to pull. Tired as he was Tom felt his spirits rising; he had triumphed, though single-handed and handicapped by having the sight of only one eye. He was hungry, thirsty and wet through but he was happy. So, as he hauled on the tow-rope of the sledge he chanted the Volga Boatman's song with words of his own choosing:

77

"Hee-ee-eve Ho!
Hee-ee-eve Ho!
Thomas Huntingdon is coming home
Thomas Huntingdon is coming home
Loaded with parcels—
Loaded with parcels
Thomas Hunting*don*—is—coming—*HOME!*"

Now there was but a hundred yards and the shack would come in sight, silhouetted against the night sky, round the next corner, passing the cave where his ambergris was stowed. Now the mosquitoes began to hum round his head, but he was used to them, and they to him, for they no longer feasted upon him so avidly as they had when first he had taken up residence. There was much for which to be thankful. One more stanza of the Volga Boatman's Song would see him there.

Chapter Ten

JEFF HOOKER'S LITTLE STRATAGEM

"HE'S coming!"

Three of the four vile men stiffened involuntarily. Jeff Hooker looked at them with contempt.

"Take it easy," he said in a low voice, "and leave the spieling to me."

He went to the medical cabinet and taking from it a hypodermic syringe which he had previously filled, he slipped it into his jacket pocket. Then he walked to the open door and stood on the veranda silhouetted against the background of golden light. Fatso, Cobbo and Pedro rose self-consciously like people who never having acted before don't know what to do with their hands.

The singing grew louder and more triumphant:

"Thomas Huntingdon is coming——" It stopped dead as the singer rounded the corner and saw what was there.

"Hullo there!" said Jeff in his heartiest of voices.

"Who are you? And where the blazes did you come from?" asked Tom.

"Shipwrecked mariners, Mister. Cast up last night. Seeing as you were away we took the liberty of moving in out of that rain."

"You're welcome", said Tom. He dropped the sledge tow-rope and moved forward with outstretched hand. "I'm Tom Huntingdon", he said.

Jeff took his hand and clapped him on the back.

"Come and meet the boys," he said genially, "they're rough but they're ready."

Tom moved forward, blinking in the light of the lamps. As he did so he felt a thump and a pricking sensation.

"What the dickens?" He staggered.

"Take it easy, Mister." Jeff Hooker's voice seemed to be coming from a long way off.

"What d'you think you're doing?" The room was going round. The four faces, bearded and unkempt were coming closer and closer. In the drawer of his desk was a revolver. "Excuse me", he said and pitched forward. They caught him gently and laid him on the floor.

Fatso passed a dirty rag over his face.

"Gee!" he said, "that was mighty quick! Went out like a light." He bent over the unconscious figure which had begun to snore stertorously.

"Is he all right?" asked Cobbo.

Jeff held up the hypodermic syringe. "He's only had the dose written on the bottle", he said carelessly.

"How long will he be out?" asked Fatso.

"Maybe an hour, maybe two", answered Jeff. "We'd better get weaving. Pedro, you and Cobbo go down and launch the boat—take that sledge of provisions with you—they'll come in real handy. When it's all ready bring the sledge back and we'll take one filled with us."

The two men detailed went out into the night, carrying a powerful torchlight which they had found in the shack.

"Worked like a charm", said Jeff more to himself than to Fatso who stood scratching his mosquito bites and looking puzzled. "What's eating you, Fatso—besides the skeeters?" he asked. Fatso edged himself so as to put the table between them.

"What's your game, Jeff?" he asked. "What's the idea of our clearing out of this place? What are you up to?"

Jeff slapped a piece of paper on the table.

"Didn't I tell you?" he demanded. "There's a coast-guard cutter due here tomorrow. If they find us here we'll be whipped off to San Cristobal and shipped home as distressed seamen. It's dead logic. So what do we do. Just clear out to Little Palmelo 'til they've gone and then come back and go on collecting this here ambergris until we've got enough to make it worth while."

"Then, next time the coastguard comes he'll tell 'em what we did to him", said Fatso.

Jeff smiled scornfully. "D'you have to be told everything twice?" he mocked. "He'll be 'out' again when they arrive and smelling to high heaven of rum. So he can't talk and they think he's drunk. See?"

Fatso looked at him curiously. "Sounds a bit too smooth for me", he said. "You wouldn't double-cross me, would you, Jeff?"

Jeff grinned and gave the conventional answer. "I would if I could", he said lightly. "How d'you think I can? We're all in this together."

"I don't know," said Fatso, "but if you are thinking on those lines go easy, Mister. Pedro wouldn't take kindly to any little thing like that."

"Thanks for the warning, pal," said Jeff, "but you didn't ought to judge other people's motives by your own. I'm on the level."

He tapped the gun in his belt. "And don't *you* think up any funny business", he said. "If you guys want to come out of this situation healthy *and* wealthy you stick to me. I'm the thinking part of this outfit. You gotta trust me. See?"

"That's just what worries me", said Fatso. He peered down at the unconscious Tom.

"One thing I won't stand for", he said. "I'm a civilised American, not a primitive Limey. Don't you try and rub that guy out. He's done us no harm. And I want to die a natural death, not in the electric chair. Savvy?"

"Your sentiments do you justice, Fatso", said Jeff. "Give me a hand with the patient. I can hear the sledge coming."

The motor-boat was perilously low in the water when they were all aboard, complete with the unconscious Tom, and a varied assortment of stores. Fatso ever the nervous one, at once objected.

"I reckon it's unsafe", he said, as he gingerly lowered himself into the bows.

Jeff shone the torchlight and noticed the greatly reduced freeboard. Then he examined the petrol tank, and topped it up from a drum which Tom always kept handy.

"What do you think, Cobbo?" he asked. "Care to risk it?"

Cobbo shook his head. "It's only five miles, isn't it?" he said. "How's about making two trips of it? You take me and the stiff (he indicated the unconscious Tom), and come back for the other two?"

Jeff hesitated for a moment, and then agreed reluctantly.

"You're right", he said. "Out you get, Pedro and Fatso!"

"O.K.," said Fatso, "and whilst you're away I'll rustle up some more stuff—we might as well live well. Come'n, Pedro."

Together they stood watching the motor-boat gliding out of the Cove, saw it turn in the first rays of the rising moon and set out for Little Palmelo Island.

"I could use a drink," said Fatso, "let's go search!"

They climbed the hill again, and as they rounded the last bend Fatso let out a grunt of surprise.

"See that!" he said.

"Jeff's left the lights on." Pedro swore softly under his breath.

"'Tis not like the Captain to be so forgetful", he said.

"Very strange." They moved forward quickly into the lighted shack.

"D'ye know somp'n?" said Fatso, seizing a bottle and raising it to his lips. "I figure that Jeff's not told us all he knows. He's cooking somp'n up." He passed the bottle over to Pedro who wiped the neck carefully before taking a swig.

"Jeff's a clever man," he said presently, "but even a clever man forgets sometimes. Trouble with you, Fatso, you not clever, only suspeecious. What you worry for?"

Fatso picked up the paper on which was typed the letter which Jeff had shown them concerning the arrival of the coastguard cutter, reading it carefully as if to try and decipher a hidden meaning in the simple words. It was headed: "Office of Coast Guard, San Cristobal" and was written in English.

"Dear Mr. Huntingdon" [it ran],

"I intend to carry out my monthly inspection of your island tomorrow, Friday. Please be present.

Yours with compliments—"

The signature was illegible.

Fatso shook his head.

"Why does the Chief of Police write in English, you tell me that?"

Pedro grinned. "Maybe dis guy Huntingdon not speak Spanish, hey?"

"Or maybe—dis guy Hooker not write Spanish?" said

Fatso unconsciously copying Pedro's voice. "Maybe the Chief of Police not coming at all. Maybe there is no Chief of Police?"

He reached for the bottle and took another swig. Whatever was in it was very strong stuff. Already the lights were jumping before his eyes.

"Say, what is this stuff?" he said thickly. He peered at the label: "Alcohol—thass all right then." He took another swig.

"What'll Chief Police say when he doesn't find anyone here—you tell me that"

Pedro scratched his head—"We ask Skipper—hey! don't drink all that—I want some more."

"D'ye know somp'n—I don't like dagoes, and that goes for you", said Fatso rising from his stool and staggering towards Pedro.

Pedro fingered his knife. "Have a little care," he said pleasantly, "or I cut you t'roat a little piece. Gimme that bottle!"

"Take it then!"

Fatso hurled it in the general direction of Pedro, but the pure alcohol which Tom always used for preserving his specimens had done its work swiftly and well. The bottle flew wide, hit the wall and burst into a thousand fragments. Pedro gave a snarl of rage and pulled out his knife. If Fatso had not at that moment collapsed on to the floor that might have been his last moment. As it was Pedro contented himself with kicking the monstrous body as it lay there, and then went in search of fresh supplies of drink.

When Jeff returned an hour later both men were dead to the world.

For a moment or two the idea might have passed through his mind of taking advantage of their helpless condition to dispose of them for all time. The temptation was great, but Jeff Hooker was not of a murderous disposition. He was a gambler who liked to live excitingly, and though he would cheerfully have robbed a widow of her last mite, and had often perjured himself, he drew the line at killing. He told himself he wouldn't enjoy the numerous deceptions he was about to practise with a sin like that on his conscience. So, with many an oath, he dragged each "corpse" separately and loaded them one at a time on Tom Huntingdon's sledge. As he was about to pull them down to the water he recollected that it had been foolish of him to have left the lights on. A more astute pair than Pedro and Fatso might have taken him up on that. As it was they were in no condition to think logically, if at all.

Fatso and Pedro began to come to as Little Palmelo Island loomed up ahead. In this they were assisted by Jeff who swilled their faces with sea-water. Presently they sat up groaning, and holding their heads. Ashore a small lantern gleamed where Cobbo and his still unconscious prisoner were camped.

"Say," said Fatso, "what's going on?"

Pedro held his aching head. "Someone's hit me with sand-bag—I'll swear it!"

Jeff stood silently in the cockpit coaxing the motor-boat into shallow water. Then he took the engine out of gear and allowed the boat to glide in until the keel just grated on the beach.

"Piccadilly Circus!" he called. "All change!" As the two fuddled objects rose swaying he struck each of them a neat little buffet in the solar plexus, and as they doubled up he pitched them over the gunwale into the shallow water and revving up his engine put it into "full astern" before they had time to catch hold of the boat.

"Say!" Cobbo's voice floated plaintively over the water. "What's the idea?"

Jeff contented himself with a loud derisive laugh as he turned the boat round and sped back to Tuna Cove.

When the morning came, he reflected, Tom Huntingdon would be able to answer Cobbo's question.

Chapter Eleven

MAROONED! (I)

DAWN was breaking as Tom began to come out of his stupor. The effects of the injection wore off in waves; one moment everything was clear, and the next his brain became submerged in swirling mists of languor. He felt weak, relaxed and unable to worry.

Beside him lay three inanimate objects, two of them snoring to high heaven. They were dirty and unshaven but there was something helpless about their attitudes. Tom tried to raise himself and discovered that his wrists and ankles were bound. "This is a dream," he said out loud, "or is it?"

The thinnest member of the trio whom Tom soon learned to call Cobbo answered immediately.

"It's no dream, mate. You might call it a nightmare, but it's no dream. We're marooned, you along with us, on this 'ere island, by that dirty double-crossing son of Satan—Jeff Hooker."

"I see", said Tom, though he didn't at all. He lay back on the shingle and felt a fresh wave of languor flooding his senses.

Cobbo stood up shading his eyes towards the rising sun. Then he went over to Tom and untied his bonds.

"Now I'm awake there's no need for these", he said. "Purely precautionary, Mister", he said apologetically.

Tom didn't move. "You needn't have bothered," he said thickly, "that injection has made me as weak as a kitten."

He turned over, stretched his cramped arms and legs and went off to sleep again.

"That's a cool customer", said Cobbo. He turned with a look of disgust to the other two sleeping figures. They weren't going to be a lot of use for some little time. Then he went and examined the heap of stores which had been unloaded on the first motor-boat ferry-trip. There was everything there to support life, which was just as well, for although the island appeared to be teeming with potential food they had no firearms between the four of them. Pedro's knife seemed to be the only lethal weapon. Perhaps it would be better if there were none, for the present anyhow. A man like Pedro who had drunk himself insensible might be an awkward customer when he first came to. Quietly Cobbo tiptoed back to where the Spaniard lay, and turning him over removed the weapon. This he concealed under a rock. Then, feeling very thirsty, he went in search of water. There must be plenty about for the vegetation was lush and a number of stunted trees were clustered with oranges. If one had to be cast away on an island, he reflected, this one seemed to be very suitable. He plucked some fruit and devoured it greedily before going inland in search of water. He hadn't far to go before he found a dark-coloured pool, not attractive but reassuring. With food and water on hand the immediate worries were over. He bent down and sampled the water—it was muddy to taste and far from pleasant so he decided to look around for something better. Across the pool he could hear the faint tinkle of running water—a legacy of last night's storm, no doubt. The quickest way there would be a straight line using those curious humps of rock as stepping-stones. The regularity and smoothness of those domed shaped objects led him in thought to the possibility of the island being inhabited. If so Mister Hooker

88

had better look out for himself, revolver or no revolver. Revenge might not have to wait as long as it had appeared likely when Jeff Hooker had left them stranded.

The first stepping-stone was some four feet or so out in the pool. Cobbo took a jump and landed neatly on its centre. He balanced there for a moment, then to his astonishment the thing he was standing on began to move. He almost flew through the air as he leapt for safety at the next stepping-stone which suddenly submerged as he arrived. He fell heavily on his face in the water, and when he had picked himself up found that he was only up to his knees in it. He found also that the "stepping-stone" had risen a few feet distant and a large scaly head—which reminded him of the portrait he'd once seen of a famous author—was looking at him with a sort of reproachful stare. No one since he had been a boy at school had ever looked so disapprovingly at him. The head belonged to an enormous turtle (or was it a tortoise?) and the other "stepping-stones" were now showing their disapproval of this clumsy stranger's actions as they slowly backed away from him. Cobbo grinned. No wonder the water hadn't tasted so good! These were real monsters— he remembered now that they were among the list of animals that Senor Pontivecchi had ordered. Galapagos Turtles! That was it!

He soon found the waterfall and gave himself a good freshening up. On the way back he encounted a turtle which was comparatively small. Swiftly he bent down and seizing the creature by its shell capsized it. It looked quite pathetic lying on its back and Cobbo had no immediate designs on its safety. He wanted the turtle for another purpose. Half dragging and half lifting the awkward specimen he reached the spot where Fatso lay dreaming and turning the turtle the right way up pointed it in the direction of Fatso's face. The creature moved forward like a gigantic mechanical toy, its limbs jerking awkwardly and its head held up in that peculiarly supercilious manner. Obviously very short-sighted it did not see that it was approaching a live creature and plodded towards Fatso like the ploughman in the poem—on his weary way. At the same time Cobbo tossed a pebble into Fatso's open mouth. He snorted, half choked and opened his eyes. For a moment he kept them open and then disbelieving what they revealed shut them again.

Tom Huntingdon was awake and enjoying the comedy. He, of course, knew all about these ancient animals who lived to tremendous ages, some of them being three centuries old. He knew they were harmless but Fatso did not. Moreover Fatso had a guilty conscience. He had drunk himself insensible and he knew what happened to people who did that sort of thing. They got the horrors! They saw things which were not really there! Just like the Thing he'd thought he'd seen. He opened his eyes and saw again the wrinkled visage glaring with equal distaste at his own unkempt appearance. This must be the horror of all horrors!

With a piercing yell he leapt up and began to run with surprising speed, considering his massive bulk.

Cobbo held his sides with mirth. Even Tom found enough energy to raise a smile and Pedro waking up at that moment soon became aware of the joke and joined in.

The sound of the laughter brought Fatso to an abrupt halt; he turned and this time was sufficiently awake to realise that he had not been "seeing things".

With a shamefaced smirk he returned to the group while the turtle with its nose well up went back to its companions and told them that there was a party of ill-bred monkeys down by the shore.

With a piercing yell he leapt up and began to run with
surprising speed, considering his massive bulk.

Tom Huntingdon was not easily scared of anything. His experiences in the war, the hardships and the dangers he'd endured at the hands of a ruthless savage enemy had left their mark. Nothing that could happen to him after that was likely to be worth taking seriously. As the lassitude in his mind and limbs gradually wore off he began to take an interest in the peculiar situation in which he now found himself. Moreover the comedy which he had just witnessed had told him much about the characters of the "three musketeers", as he privately named them. Pedro, Cobbo and Fatso had been double-crossed by the D'Artagnan of the party—that much was clear. But why? And where did he, Tom, come in in all this?

He leaned with his back against a smooth rock and revelled in the sunshine which warmed him comfortably and removed the stiffness of his limbs. The three musketeers had withdrawn beyond earshot and were in close confabulation while they knocked up a breakfast of tea and canned-beef stew. By the way they gestured and nodded in his direction it was clear that he was the subject of this debate. Presently they rose from their squatting postures round the fire and brought their breakfasts with them. Cobbo handed him a mug of tea and a plate of stew which he accepted and set about consuming with a will. When he had finished he fished in his pocket for his pipe, found it and his tobacco to be intact, and filling it borrowed a light from Cobbo and puffed blissfully in silence. The three men looked at him and then at each other in a way which reminded him of an occasion when he had surprised three small boys helping themselves to his strawberries. They looked thoroughly guilty and quite miserable.

"Cheer up", he said. "It's a lovely day for a picnic."

Cobbo, lean, wiry and every inch a free-booting type,

nodded approvingly. "You're a cool one and no mistake", he said.

Fatso, corpulent and possessed of many chins wiped his mouth on the back of his hand before feeling in his jeans for a stick of chewing-gum which he proceeded to masticate with that peculiar rotary movement of the jaws effected by his countrymen.

Pedro, his head still throbbing from the previous night's excesses, sat muttering things to himself in Spanish. Whether they were prayers or maledictions it was difficult to discover.

"All comfortable?" asked Tom blandly. They were becoming more and more like naughty boys as he looked at them. It was clear that they bore him no ill-will, on the contrary, they had come to him for help.

"Well now," said Tom, "I think I'm entitled to an explanation."

They looked at each other and then by mutual consent Cobbo did the talking.

He told Tom everything that had happened, from the time of the start of the ill-fated expedition to the discovery of the letter for the Chief of the Police and the decision by Jeff Hooker to evacuate the island until the danger was past.

"Maybe you don't know it," concluded Cobbo, "but there's some pretty valuable stuff lying about the beaches there, it's called ambergris."

"Oh yes", said Tom. "I know all about that. And so, I fancy, does your Mr. Hooker. In fact I suspect that he's discovered that for the past months I've been collecting it against the day when I return to civilisation. Did he tell you that?" They shook their heads glumly. "Did he tell you that I'm expecting another visitor any day now?"

Again they shook their heads.

"By the way," said Tom lazily, "that letter from the Chief of Police is a fake. I never had one. Hooker probably typed it himself on my typewriter. What was the signature?"

"Couldn't read it", said Cobbo.

"Quite so", said Tom pleasantly.

"What I want to know," said Cobbo, "is what he expects to gain by marooning us on this here island. Jeff Hooker never did nothing for no object."

"He clever man," said Pedro, "when I see him I cut his t'roat a little." His hand strayed to his belt. "Caramba!" he muttered, "my knife—it is lost."

"Just as well", said Cobbo with something of a wink in the direction of Tom. "This gentleman here, who has put up with a great deal from us already might get wrong ideas in his head if you go around talking like that, Pedro."

"All the same I cut his t'roat", said Pedro in a sulky voice. "You see!"

"What do you figure Jeff's up to, Mister?" Fatso removed his chewing-gum, examined it with interest and put it back in his mouth.

"Well," said Tom as he knocked out his pipe, "I've been trying to put myself in his position. Here I am—that is, here is Jeff Hooker alone on the island with a considerable quantity of ambergris. He has succeeded in eliminating his three bonny friends—that's you—and myself. His visitors are to be a party of men and children who are sailing for pleasure round the world in a yacht which is skippered by an old shipmate of mine in the British Navy—a Commander Firebrace who has been invited to spend Christmas with me."

"I don't get it," said Fatso, "the first thing this Commander-guy will want to know is where you are."

"Ah," said Tom, "I'm beginning to see how things are likely to go. Clearly Jeff Hooker is a master-strategist."

"He's an unprintable double-crossing devil", said Cobbo without heat.

"He's clever, dat man", said Pedro. "Someday I cut his t'roat from here to here."

"I still don't get it", said Fatso.

"Well," said Tom, "it's like this. Being alone on an island is something of a trial of patience. If one is not very careful one begins to allow oneself to deteriorate." His eyes wandered over the filthy clothes and features of his companions before he went on.

"So," he continued, "I have been in the habit of writing a complete diary of my day-to-day life and keeping copies of all my correspondence. It would not take very long for a man of Jeff Hooker's calibre to go through my records and to discover one very important thing about Commander Firebrace. He wrote to me in reply to my letter and said that although he recollected my name when we were together in H.M.S. *Borealis* he wouldn't know me from Adam—he has no recollection of my appearance except that I have told him that I have this—he pointed to the black patch over his eye.

"I get it," said Cobbo, "he's going to pretend to be you —and he'll persuade this 'Pommy' Commander to take him—and the ambergris—away out of here."

"That's what I intended to do, gentlemen."

"The dirty dingo!" said Cobbo. "When's this boat due?"

"Any day now", said Tom. "We will have an excellent view of her arrival from here when she does come."

Pedro ground his teeth and repeated his intentions.

Cobbo pounded his knee with his fist. "We're a proper lot of Charleys—that's us."

Fatso turned an appealing face to the man he'd helped to kidnap. "Isn't there anything we can do, Mister? Are you going to sit there and allow that so-and-so to get away with all your stuff?"

"What do you suggest?" asked Tom. "I wouldn't advise trying to cross that five miles of water, even on a raft; the sharks in these parts are a hungry lot. You might try lighting a bonfire on the top of that hill. It might attract attention, and again it might not."

"You don't seem to be caring very much, Mister", said Fatso. "Maybe you know somep'n you haven't told us?"

Tom smiled.

"Yes, I do", he said. "You tell me something, Fatso. This Jeff Hooker. Is he a thorough sort of chap? I mean if he decided to impersonate me would he take a lot of trouble, or would he just bluff his way through?"

"Bluff's his middle name, Mister."

"Then," said Tom placidly, "there's quite a hope."

Cobbo leaned forward eagerly. "Go on, mate. Spill it!"

"I don't think I will," said Tom, "it could make no difference to our chances if I did. But one thing I will say for you to ponder on. It goes something like this: 'If you want to know what's going to happen in the future you should look at the past.'"

"I don't get it", said Fatso mechanically.

"It doesn't matter whether you do or not," said Tom, "but if Jeff Hooker knows that, he'll be worrying a lot." He rose.

"It's time I had a wash", he said. "In the meantime, gentlemen, you'd do well to erect a beacon on the top of yonder hill. It may be your only chance of rescue and again it may not."

"He's a cool one", said Cobbo uneasily. "A mighty cool one."

Chapter Twelve

THE GREEN SAILORS ARRIVE

WHENEVER *Rag Doll* was at sea on a Sunday Uncle George held a little Church Service, unless the weather conditions made it impossible to do so. This was a habit he'd formed as the captain of a submarine, and one to which once his crew had become accustomed was regarded as a very necessary reminder of the outside world and Things beyond.

So, as *Rag Doll* careered along under the influence of a quartering breeze, rolling in a way which reminded them all of their long crossing of the Atlantic the entire crew gathered in the cockpit, sang a couple of hymns, listened to Uncle George's choice of a Lesson which he invariably chose from the more exciting parts of the Books of Kings, and said a prayer for their friends and relations on the other side of the world. It was a short affair, but none the less impressive, for whilst they repeated the familiar words which were being said on that day in so many countries their thoughts travelled back across the four and a half thousand miles which separated them from their homes and they wondered what was going on there. Eleven a.m. for *Rag Doll* meant that in England it was already dark—the curtains would be drawn at home, the fire burning brightly and the old people would be just about having their second cups of tea. Daddy would probably be saying that the present-day crumpets were not what they used to be. It was either raining or very foggy.

It was difficult to imagine oneself back in that other world of draughts and colds and flu and measles and Teddy Boys and the television and school. For six days now no evidence of other human beings had been sighted. Their world was inhabited by three men, four Green Sailors, and all the wild things one could imagine—hundreds and thousands of miles of ocean stretched in all directions. Probably the course which they were steering was making a brand-new track across the earth's surface which no other vessel had ever exactly followed. They were breaking trail, a trail which left nothing for others to follow except an occasional bottle, in which was placed one of Binnie's more dramatic compositions. Perhaps, long after the Greens had grown up, married and had children some person wandering on a beach in search of ambergris or other treasures would find these messages from the past: perhaps, thought Binnie, as she mentally composed another one while Uncle George's voice boomed above the ceaseless swishing of the waves, perhaps in a million years from now a space-man from Mars or beyond would be the first to read her letter—"To all whom it may concern. I, B. Green, in position fifty miles due east of the Galapagos, a member of the crew of the ketch *Rag Doll*, do send out this message to you—a Merry Christmas and a prosperous New Year."

—"be with us all, this day and for ever more—Amen." The Service was over.

There was a little silence among the "congregation" before they went about their business: Mary to the galley—assisted by the cook's mate of the day—in this instance, Loopy—Uncle George and Mark to pore over the chart of the Galapagos and the pages of the "Pilot for South American Waters," Binnie and Ben to actually write the message which she had already made up and Ted at the wheel steering the course which would take them to San Cristobal.

There was a general Sunday-ish feeling about the day.

Uncle George had frequently remarked on this phenomenon. The Sabbath calm, he said, was common enough wherever a sailor went. One awoke to it, and in harbour one would hear the church-bells and the little other sounds which on a working day were swamped by the hum of industry. Here, at sea, the wind was certainly lighter than it had been for the past two days and dead ahead were the tell-tale fluffy white clouds, the first indication of the existence of land which they were rapidly approaching.

As Ben struck eight bells which proclaimed the hour of noon the first living evidence of the nearness of land appeared. A cloud of birds came down to welcome the strangers from another world. Three days had elapsed since the last of their followers from the continent had turned back. Now, once more the air was filled with diving, skimming and hovering birds, and huge green sea-turtles popped up to swell the chorus of welcoming noises as they filled their lungs anew to the accompaniment of melancholy deep-breathing puffs. Meanwhile the under-water escort was not being idle. The presence of the Boobies and other smaller birds seemed to galvanise the life of the small fishes which skimmed on the surface of the waters, hunted from below and from above. Great sword-fish and other many-coloured beauties leapt in pursuit of lesser fry. The Sabbath calm did not apply to that community. Eat or be eaten was the watchword. So it had always been and would continue to the world's end unless the balance of nature was interfered with by man-made devices.

Now the afternoon breeze freshened to bring this stage of their journey to a swift conclusion and a strong tidal stream gave them almost a quarter as much again of their speed through the water. Within a few hours of the arrival of the birds high land was sighted dead ahead and Uncle George shook hands with Mark with a gesture of mutual congratulation. Without a doubt it was San Cristobal which was rising out of the sea at a tremendous pace. Now it was a race against time to reach their appointed anchorage in Wreck Bay before total darkness. *Rag Doll* seemed to know that dispatch was necessary as with every stitch of canvas she could carry she soared through the steep little waves towards the westering sun.

By half-past five that evening they had passed under the lee of the northern shores of the island and found themselves almost becalmed. Aunt Bertha was started up, the sails were furled and course was laid for Wreck Bay.

It was very dark when they arrived and no lights were visible on the land, so as soon as soundings of under ten fathoms were reached Uncle George dropped anchor and *Rag Doll* lay rolling gently in the swell while from the shore came the weird noises of the tropical night.

Chapter Thirteen

"NO FUNNY BUSINESS——!"

THE next day dawned fine and warm, the Trade Wind having lost much of its vigour. As soon as it was light enough to see, Uncle George weighed anchor and brought *Rag Doll* alongside the somewhat dilapidated pier where a few natives of the island lounged and looked at the visitors with a complete lack of curiosity.

The Green Sailors were naturally anxious to go ashore and to explore this strange and somewhat sinister island, but Uncle George said no—not until permission had been given by the local authority. And it was well that he did so, for it would have suited Colonel Gaspardo very well to have had a chance to wield his powers as Chief of Police and to put the vessel under temporary arrest.

In countries situated on the Equator things do not happen very quickly, and woe-betide those people who do not possess the necessary patience to await developments. This was particularly galling to the crew of *Rag Doll* who had urged their good ship along at her top speed and now were obliged to sit on deck waiting.

It was well after noon when a cloud of dust appeared at the top of the nearest hill, up which wound a primitive road. The cloud was formed by a posse of soldiers, rough half-castes far from smartly dressed, unshaven and unkempt, but mounted on magnificent beasts whose harness and equipment were very picturesque. They were armed with small carbines which they carried slung over their backs. They came galloping down the hill in rather a menacing manner and dismounting with a flourish tethered their steeds in the manner with which the Greens had become acquainted by the medium of television "Westerns", and then sat down in a row and lit cigarettes.

Ted Tottle, who knew a little Spanish wished them good morning and asked who was the senior officer? To this they shrugged and indicated that their officer would come later. "How much later?" inquired Ted. They shrugged again and replied with the traditional "*Quién sabe?*" (who knows?). They were not exactly hostile but they were far from friendly and fingered their weapons significantly as if to say "No funny business". The Greens watched these people with increasing discomfort, for this was hardly the welcome they had anticipated.

After what seemed to be an eternity another cloud of dust appeared on the hill-top. The posse stubbed out their cigarettes and stood up as an antiquated Ford car of a vintage known as a "T" model came snaking down the track. Seated in the back, immaculately dressed, was an officer. The old motor-buggy turned on to the jetty and screeched to a slithering halt about six inches from the end just when the Greens had decided that it was going to come aboard *Rag Doll*.

Uncle George had donned a yachting coat and cap and was wearing a tie for the occasion. He had sensed that the officials of this outpost of civilization might be inclined towards pomposity and was prepared for the sake of good relations to meet them more than half-way. Colonel Gaspardo —for it was he—stood for a while on the jetty, looking at the visitors and twisting his starboard moustachio. Then he stepped aboard with his hand at the salute. Unfortunately his spurs caught up on a projecting part of the jetty so that

Unfortunately his spurs caught up on a projecting part of
the jetty so that instead of making a dignified arrival, he fell
heavily into the arms of Uncle George.

instead of making a dignified arrival, he fell heavily into the arms of Uncle George.

"Welcome aboard, sir", said the Commander with as much enthusiasm as he could muster. The Colonel recovered his balance and turned sharply round to see if anyone was laughing. Fortunately no one was.

"Will you come below, sir?"

The Colonel looked at the open hatch and then at his spurs.

"No thank you", he said in his excellent English. "Perhaps later, after we have finished the official side of the businesses." He pulled himself up to his full height and adopting an official—if not officious—voice he said: "Your name is Jeffery Hooker. You are a British subject. These two men I know of"—he indicated Ted and Loopy—"but where is the fourth and who are these children? They were not aboard when you sailed from Bueno Ventura—did you find them? Answer me—no shilly-shilly!"

Uncle George shook his head. "I think there is some misunderstanding," he said.

"No," said the Colonel, "there is no misunderstanding. My information is that you are agents of Senor Pontivecchi, that you have made an arrangement to visit a certain person on Palmelo Island and that your object in coming here is to steal the protected wild-beasts——" He broke off and a puzzled look came over his face. "This is a very small craft—where did you intend to put your cargo—answer me that—and no shilly-shilly?"

"Look!" said Uncle George: "allow me to clear this matter, please!" He dived below and returned with the ship's papers, the permit which he had been at such pains to procure in Balboa, and the passports of every member of the crew. The Colonel took each exhibit as if it were hot to the touch, examined it and handed it back. A look of disappointment and frustration came into his eyes as he finished the examination, but his sense of dignity stood him in good stead. He clicked his spurs together and bowed.

"I will admit, Senor Commandatore there has been a mixture. One thousand apologies and welcome to the Galapagos!"

He turned to the watching troops and addressed them in his own language. They went to their horses and galloped away.

"Now, Senor," he said, "if you will permit me to remove these unsuitable excrescences—perhaps I will avail myself of your kind offer. It is thirsty work, making mistakes, eh?"

"Splendid," said Uncle George, "and now allow me to present the members of my crew——"

"Colonel Enrico Gaspardo", interposed the visitor. They all shook hands and then having removed his spurs the Colonel was taken below and entertained, and as he consumed glass after glass of wine he became friendlier and friendlier. "You will all stay here as my guests—it is the Festive Season", he declared.

"That's exceedingly kind," said Uncle George, "but we have already accepted an invitation from an old friend—perhaps you know him? Doctor Huntingdon on Palmelo Island."

The Colonel's eyes glinted momentarily. "Yes, I know a great deal about Senor Huntingdon, but not that he was a doctor, and I was aware that he was expecting visitors. Beyond that there has been a certain confusion. Our Intelligence system has gone all hay-cock—is that the correct term?"

"Nearly", said Uncle George. The Colonel picked up the Commander's passport and studied it awhile.

"You have never met nor heard speak of Jeffery Hooker?" he inquired.

"Definitely not."

"Nor Senor Pontivecchi?"

"Absolutely positively not."

"Good!"

He rose to go and then in the manner of all good detectives he asked the "64 thousand dollar" question at the moment when his suspect was most likely to be off his guard.

"Senor Commandatore," he said, "you are free and welcome to visit any island under my jurisdiction. You will give my best wishes to the Doctor, will you not?"

"Certainly, I will."

"Good. Tell me, Senor, what task is it that Doctor Huntingdon wishes you to undertake for him?"

Uncle George looked thoroughly puzzled by this question until he remembered the cryptic reference to such a possibility in Huntingdon's letter.

"You mean the D.D.T.?" he asked, "I have about ten pounds of it, as well as other stores which he wrote for."

"Nothing else?" asked the Colonel.

"Nothing that I know of."

"That is a different matter," said the Colonel significantly. "Allow me to give you some advice, Senor. If you have plans to meet this Jeffery Hooker—abandon them. You play square with me and I play fair with you. A nod is as good as a horse to a blind wink. And remember——" he paused dramatically.

"I am the master of everything here. No funny business, if you please."

．　　　．　　　．

When he had gone Uncle George scratched his head.

"I couldn't agree more," he said, "no funny business. I must have a heart-to-heart talk with Tom Huntingdon. That Colonel chap's looking for trouble. And we are a long way away from friends!"

Chapter Fourteen

"MEMORY PLAYS STRANGE TRICKS..."

IT was nearly dark as *Rag Doll* came abreast of the south-west corner of Palmelo Island and turned into the channel which separated the former from its junior partner where the smoke of a small fire was rising spasmodically in the evening air.

"Curious that", said Uncle George. "If I were in the Wild West I would fancy that Redskins were broadcasting the six o'clock news. I understood that Little Palmelo Island was uninhabited. Harden in your sheets, chaps, and clear away the anchor!"

Down went the helm and *Rag Doll* swung quickly to starboard, revelling in the calm water and off-shore breeze which brought with it wonderful scents, the like of which the land-starved mariners had never before experienced. The last mile or so was something of a triumphal progress; Palmelo was giving a royal reception to its visitors. Flocks of birds screamed overhead, great sea-lions roared their welcome, and the sea was alive with jumping tuna. Ashore a solitary light gleamed, while down on the rocky foreshore a man was waving.

"This," said Loopy, as he and the remainder of the crew waved back; "this is much more like it."

The next minutes passed in a flash. Down came the sails, Mark standing, lead-line in hand and sounding as the yacht glided in towards the shore. Uncle George blissfully smoking his pipe and feeling as expectant of good things to come as he had been otherwise at San Cristobal, listened to the sounds of cheerful bustle against the background of wild-life noises, and felt that it had all been very well worth while. Ashore, an old shipmate was no doubt as expectant as himself. There's a saying in the Navy that there's no ship like the last ship, which is another way of putting the words—"distance lends enchantment". Uncle George's recollections of that commission in H.M.S. *Borealis* were wholly pleasant; if anything had gone wrong in those far-off days it was long since forgotten. What remained in his memory was a warm feeling of happy days. He tried to conjure up a picture of Tom Huntingdon's personal appearance, but failed. Memory plays odd tricks—he remembered the name so well, but of the face—nothing remained.

"By the Mark, five", shouted the leadsman.

"Anchor's ready for letting go!" Ben's squeaky voice came clearly in the evening air. Ted and Loopy were rolling up the great mainsail into a neat sausage. Mary and Binnie were at the engine controls. The touch of a button started Aunt Bertha.

"Slow ahead", ordered Uncle George.

"Slow ahead, sir!" came Binnie's cocky little voice. Uncle George smiled. It was close on a thousand miles since Binnie had called him "Sir"—a sign of great condescension on her part.

"Deep four!"

"Stop the engine. Stand by!" There was a moment's pause: even the birds seemed to be listening.

"By the Mark, three!"

"Let go! Half speed astern!"

With a roar and a rattle the anchor and cable went down and *Rag Doll* shivered as Aunt Bertha sprang to life again to pull her up. In a few minutes it was finished.

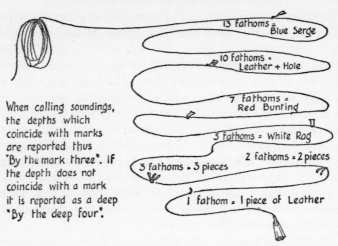

When calling soundings, the depths which coincide with marks are reported thus 'By the mark three". If the depth does not coincide with a mark it is reported as a deep 'By the deep four".

13 fathoms = Blue Serge
10 fathoms = Leather + Hole
7 fathoms = Red Bunting
5 fathoms = White Rag
2 fathoms = 2 pieces
3 fathoms = 3 pieces
1 fathom = 1 piece of Leather

Hardly had they secured cable and started to hoist out the boat which had replaced the one lost in the hurricane, back there in the Caribbean, than a battered old dinghy put off from the shore and came alongside with something of a bump. A man wearing a black patch over one eye threw up a painter, and clambered aboard.

He stood for a moment uncertainly, as if trying to make up his mind. Then, seeing Ted Tottle's magnificent beard, he moved forward with outstretched hand.

"Same old smiling face!" he said gaily. "How are you, Firebrace?" As he spoke he gained a clearer view of Ted's otherwise youthful figure and drew back, putting a hand up to his blacked-out eye.

"Hullo there!"

Uncle George's hearty voice settled the matter. The newcomer turned quickly. "For a moment," he said, "I mistook—I can't see very well in this light." He grasped Uncle George's hand.

"I'd have known you anywhere", he added. "How are you, after all these years, sir? Not a day older, as I recollect you."

"My dear fellow", said Uncle George. "Here we are, on schedule. Come on down and have a drink! Moor his boat up, someone, and come down to be introduced where we can see each other. Mary, switch the lights on!"

They went below, leaving Binnie and Ben to complete the mooring up of Tom Huntingdon's dinghy. Ben jumped in and searched under the after thwart for a sternfast, but found nothing. Binnie found a short line and passed it to him. As he rove it through a ring bolt in the boat's transom Ben squeaked his usual swear-word. "Jumping kangaroos!" he exclaimed; "it's all wet paint on the stern!"

"It's good to see you all." Jeff Hooker leaned back in his corner and smiled benignly on his hosts. This was going to be a piece of cake. These charming pleasure-seeking globe-trotters were so full of their own affairs and with curiosity to see the wonders of the Galapagos that the word suspicion wouldn't be in their vocabularies. "Take it easy, Jeff," he told himself, "act natural and don't rush things." Then he corrected himself: "Take it easy, *Tom*," he silently repeated, "you're Tom and don't you forget it."

"What will you drink?" asked Uncle George, beaming with true naval hospitality.

"Drop o' scotch? Anything as long as it's wet and strong. You, know mister—I mean Commander—this is a red-letter day and no mistake. I been straining my eyes for days, looking out to sea like the proverbial peninsula." He remembered his eye patch and added: "Figuratively speaking of course. I won't deny," he went on, carefully ignoring Uncle George's attentions with the whisky-bottle until the glass was well and truly loaded, "Whoa! that's more than plenty! I won't deny that I'm tired of my own company so if I talk too much you'll just have to forgive me. I guess Robinson Crusoe was a proper natterer when *he* got among his fellow creatures. Here's mud in your eye, and here's to the old *Boreelis*!" (He pronounced it as spelt.)

Uncle George raised his own glass and repeated the toast. "Borealis——"

"Oy oy!" said Jeff to himself, "so that's how it's pronounced!" He hastened to "cover up" his mistake. "Some say tomatoes and some say tomartoes," he quoted, "the sailors always called her Bor*ee*lis." He took a good swig and accepted a cheroot. "Real naval hospitality", he said. "I might have guessed it would be this way." He turned to the four Greens who, he felt, were regarding him with certain reservations.

"Well now, you young people", he said. "Don't be shy! It's only your old Uncle Tom. Shake hands, little man!" This to Ben.

Ben shook his head. "I'd better not," he said, "there's wet paint in your boat, sir. Did you know it?"

He showed his hands. "I'll just get some turps."

Jeff gasped admiring. "He's a quick one, that boy! Spotting my rather feeble attempts to smarten her up in your honour." He turned to Binnie.

"Well, young lady? Going to give your Uncle Tom a kiss?"

Binnie, who knew her *My Fair Lady*, gave the appropriate reply.

"Not bloody likely." She turned and followed Ben.

Jeff smacked his knee and roared with laughter.

"Proper up-to-date young Miss," he said, "pony-tail an' all."

Uncle George grunted. Already he was beginning to

wonder why he had felt such an urge to call on this old ship-mate; moreover something was stirring in that erratic memory of his—struggling to emerge from the depths of his subconscious mind. He thoroughly approved of Binnie's reply, but like a true host he made excuses for her.

"Hardly in the tradition of your favourite author", he said.

Jeff blinked—"We must move with the times", he said. There was a pause and Mary came in with a rush.

"Which one do you like best?" she asked, remembering what Tom Huntingdon had written in his letter.

"Come again?" said Jeff, playing for time.

Uncle George prompted him. "You said you were a devotee of Jane Austen, remember?"

"Remember Jane Austen—who wouldn't? Ho-ho! Wasn't that the piece of home-work at Swatow—or am I thinking of——" He paused waiting for a clue.

"The authoress," said Mary kindly, "you wrote and said you could recite whole chunks of her."

"Did I? So I did." Jeff took a long drink. "Careful, Tom", he said to himself. "Don't stick your neck out. These people are too interested. They don't miss a trick."

He rose and said he must be getting along.

"You must stay and eat with us", said Uncle George.

Jeff shook his head. "Work calls," he said, "I've a lot of reading and writing to do—I mustn't slack off. I'm being paid, you know."

"One for the dinghy, then?"

"There's no harm in that", said Jeff, settling down in his couch again.

"Just a wee one—a wee deoch and doris—as we say in Scotland!"

Bingo! That was it! Uncle George's thought popped

right out. Tom Huntingdon used to speak in a broad low-land Scots accent. He remembered now.

"Yes," he said as he replenished Jeff's glass, "I'd for-gotten you were from 'North of the Border'. You've lost your Scots accent."

"You don't say." Jeff's accent became the "real McCoy" for a few sentences.

"It's the sassenach company I was obliged to keep. Besides I can pick up any accent." He lapsed into broad Irish.

"A couple of months with the Paddies now and I'll be after kissing the Blarney Stone and there's no mistake."

He raised his glass again. "The top of the evening to you all!"

Ted and Loopy exchanged glances. This wasn't at all the sort of man they'd been expecting. Somehow his letter had conveyed a taciturn type who had suffered much in the war and had sought solitude in this faraway place. Yet, here he was, behaving like a third-rate music-hall comedian. He'd be telling undrawing-room stories next. Perhaps it was the drink. Uncle George was always inclined to be over-lavish in his hospitality.

Two drinks later Jeff pulled himself together.

"You've been too kind to me", he said, moving a little uncertainly towards the cockpit. "I'd better go whilst I can." He laughed. "Did I ever tell you the story of the Duchess and the umbrella—it's a scream!" His glance rested for a moment on the mutual looks which passed between Loopy and Ted—and he took warning from them.

"Not before the children, eh!" He went on deck and sniffed the air. Far away across the five-mile stretch of water—a flame was flickering on Little Palmelo Island.

Uncle George pointed it out.

114

"Ah!" said Jeff carelessly. "It's them natives. Keeps the mosquitoes away to have a fire at night." He clambered nimbly into the dinghy. "Tomorrow morning you must all come and breakfast with me. Cheery-bye!"

Uncle George watched his guest disappearing into the darkness and shook his head.

Memory could certainly play strange tricks, but—he scratched his chin and went below in search of a book. Yes! There it was in black and white:

"Discovered in 1535 by Berlanza, the Archipelago has remained with a few exceptions in its original *uninhabited* state." He closed the book. There were no "natives". "Curiouser and curiouser: said Alice," he muttered.

Jeff Hooker had spoken the truth when he had said that he was going back to work. He had suddenly realised that he'd gone into this idea of impersonating Tom Huntingdon far too lightheartedly. He sat glued to his chair looking through Tom's journals and diaries. Tomorrow he must be prepared to correct any wrong impressions he might have made—be more reserved—plead loss of memory, and refuse any further hospitality. It was too dangerous. That whisky had been very strong. Too strong in fact to go on reading. He yawned and smiled; this was exciting; he'd bluff his way through all right. He slept.

Chapter Fifteen

EXPLORATION

LIFE aboard a small sailing vessel is not exactly strenuous but all the crew are held in the bonds of discipline. Ships where there is more than one captain don't last very long—witness the loss of *Black Jack*. Such discipline in *Rag Doll* was not necessarily irksome but it was nice to get out of harness now and again, away from people who gave orders, even in the friendliest of manners. So it was that Mark and Mary informed Uncle George, Ted and Loopy that they were going to explore the island without the aid of grown-ups, and Uncle George who understood that young people can have too much of the "oldun's" company readily agreed.

No one had taken Tom Huntingdon's invitation to break-fast literally: it would be unlikely that he could have coped with such a horde. After a good tuck-in of tinned sausages and bacon, therefore, Mary packed up a satchel of food, while the others sought eagerly for shore-going footwear, floppy hats, cameras, butterfly nets and everything suitable for exploration.

Uncle George gave his instructions. They were to look out for snakes and scorpions. The large lizards were harmless and so were the sea-lions as long as they were left alone. Bathing in the sea was absolutely prohibited—the sharks were too fierce and hungry. If there was a fresh-water lake with clear water in it they could use that for swimming.

"And be back by eight bells in the afternoon watch," he concluded.

They piled into the dinghy, chattering eagerly while Uncle George planted himself in the stern and worked the outboard motor. Ted and Loopy looked a little envious as the gay little party phut-phutted ashore: they wouldn't have minded going along with the Green Sailors but perhaps it would make a nice change to be rid of the noise and bustle that always went on when they were about. They would go ashore and do a bit of exploring themselves.

In a matter of minutes the explorers were once more on dry land. Uncle George watched them plodding up the steep slope from the little jetty staggering almost as much as his guest of last night; *Rag Doll*'s motion during the past week had been pretty considerable so that the Greens had become used to balancing all the while. Now, the earth was steady but the balancing mechanisms of their brains and bodies could not at once readjust themselves. Hence the so-called "nautical roll". Uncle George watched them out of sight before returning to the yacht.

It was a beautifully warm day; the sky was flecked with white fluffy clouds which cast their shadow on the blue sea, turning it into patches of deep purple. The Greens followed a track which led them to the highest point of the island, obeying the instinct of all explorers to reach the heights, and as they steadily climbed the wild life teemed around them. Little Lizards darted across the path, larger ones scurried away much to the relief of the explorers, for they looked thoroughly savage and prehistoric. At one place they found a large brood of young iguanas—dozens of little black dragons. Knowing them to be harmless Ben suggested capturing one and keeping it on board as a pet. It seemed a good idea but as they spread out to round up the herd they

discovered that the iguanas had their own somewhat unpleasant methods of defence. They retreated into a solid
phalanx, climbing on each other's backs and facing outwards
like infantry-men of old, "forming square". Then as the
Greens approached they began to spit in unison. Considering their extreme youth and small size they were very power-
fully equipped for spitting and a barrage of unpleasant
liquid was created at a distance of several feet around them.
By common consent the Greens moved away, after an in-
effective attempt by Binnie and Ben to spit back at their
opponents. Hardly had they passed out of range than their
attention was drawn to one of the giant turtles—the Galapago. It was enormous and completely friendly, having lived
to an age at which a creature ceases to care about the minor
dangers of life. It seemed to bear no ill-will when Binnie and
Ben climbed on its back. It did not withdraw its head and
limbs as a common or garden tortoise would have done. Instead it plodded along with its passengers on top, reflecting
no doubt that when it had been a young turtle—that would
have been in Queen Anne's reign—it too had liked a ride on
its parents' backs—who had been born the year that Sir
Francis Drake circumnavigated the world.

Mark and Mary produced their cameras and obtained the
sort of snapshot which people don't believe. After the shut-
ters had clicked the ancient Galapago turned suddenly off
the path down the steep hill-side, thus causing its passengers
to tumble off its back, rolling down the slope for quite a
distance. The creature seemed to give a sort of sniff as if to
say: "That's quite sufficient. I haven't worked so hard for a
hundred years." Then it planted itself between two boulders
and withdrew from public life.

Round the next corner they sighted the lake and the
wonderful birds which rose in clouds to welcome them. It

Mark and Mary produced their cameras and obtained the
sort of snapshot which people don't believe

was breath-takingly beautiful to see such a mass of graceful creatures wheeling silently but for the sound of their powerful wings which came to the ear like strange music. For a while the birds flew round and then, having given this suitable display of acrobatics in honour of the humans they settled at the far end of the lake and went on with the business of cleaning their feathers.

"Let's bathe," said Mark, feeling the water with his fingers, "it's beautifully cool and it's as clear as crystal." He stripped off his clothes, pulled on his trunks and stepped manfully into the lake while the others watched. They had already seen many strange sights and were doubtful about the advisability of entering the water. "Come on," shouted Mark—"it's lovely!"

Then he gave a yelp of surprise not unmixed with fear and scrambled out of the water as if pursued by the Furies themselves.

"Ugh!" he panted, pointing down at his legs and feet on which a large number of black slug-like creatures had fastened. "Leaches! Blood-suckers!" He bent down and managed to pull one of the leaches off his leg; as it came away a smear of blood appeared on Mark's skin. He felt faint at the sight of it and saw the other black horrors swelling visibly as they filled themselves with his blood.

Mark had read about these leaches and knew the best way of freeing himself. "Box of matches," he said hoarsely, "light that bit of wood!"

Mary produced the matches and started a small fire with sticks and dry undergrowth while Binnie and Ben ran about in search of further fuel. When a good blaze was going Mark crawled over to it and pulled a glowing ember out of it. With it he dislodged his unwelcome visitors by touching each one with the burning end. As he did so they let go of their suction apparatus and curling up dropped off his legs and feet. They counted them—over a dozen. Mark's legs were crimson with his gore as it ran out of the little punctures in his flesh made by the leeches. He looked and felt extremely wobbly but cheered up when Mary produced her first-aid bag and stuck him up with Elastoplast.

"Anyone else for a bathe?" he asked. There were no takers. Up the hill the old Galapago put his head out and nodded. "Young fools," it said to itself, "they'll learn in a couple of centuries!"

Up the hill they went, slightly shaken by Mark's encounter with the leeches and looking warily about them for poisonous snakes and scorpions as Uncle George had suggested they should. Soon, however, their high spirits reasserted themselves and they reached the summit with a loud cheer. There in a niche of the rocky eminence they were being given a most magnificent all-round view which in all probability had only been shared by a few other people since the beginning of time. A light breeze was blowing at that height, so that the temperature was just right for picnicking. Mary produced the food and bottled orangeade and they restored themselves whilst they looked about them. To the South they could see San Cristobal, its high ground wreathed in grey clouds. To the west other islands loomed uncertainly in the dim distance, while closer still they were looking down across the five-mile channel separating them from Little Palmelo on whose peak there still lingered a wisp of smoke.

"Now where do we go?" asked Binnie when all the provisions had been consumed.

Mark scanned the contours of the high ground and espied a small well-trodden track which followed the ridge in an easterly direction. "Come on," he said, "old Huntingdon's obviously used this path a great deal. I wonder where it leads to?"

They went forward in single file, picking their way carefully least they trod in a nest of vipers, and as they went the conversation turned to the lone inhabitant of the island.

"He's not at all the sort of man I expected", said Mary.

"Or Uncle George," added Binnie, "I don't believe he is Tom Huntingdon."

"There you go again", said Mark.

"Look", he said earnestly. "This is a perfect uninhabited island—except for us and Tom H. of course. It's the nearest thing to the Garden of Eden left in this world. It belongs to the past: there are no modern inventions and the only evidence of human beings having landed here before us are those goats and look at them! Compared with the *real* animals they are a scraggy lot!"

As he spoke a pair of wild goats leapt across the path and raced wildly down the hill.

"I could stay here for ages", went on Mark dreamily. "Just think of it—there's everything here to support life: fish, fowl and even mutton. Oranges, guavas, avocado pears, just waiting to be picked. This is a perfect paradise."

"Speech!" called Ben. "You didn't say that when you were being sucked by the leeches."

"That was my silly fault," said Mark, "certainly not the leeches."

"What I want to know," said Binnie, "is what leeches live on when they haven't any blood to suck?"

"Ask the mosquitoes," suggested Mary. She spoke to her elder brother. "What are you trying to say?" she asked.

Mark pondered a while. "I don't want to think that

we've sailed all this distance to this wonderful place only to find that we've once more landed ourselves with a crook."

"And you think that we have?"

"Yes."

"Oh dear!" said Mary. "Anyhow, it's nothing to do with Trogoff and his merry men—they're all either dead or in prison. And I can't see what one man can do against all of us. So I agree with you, Mark. Let's enjoy our picnic and forget about crooks and smugglers."

"And look where you're going!" shouted Ben. It was well that he did so, for the path had suddenly come to an end, and they found themselves standing on the sheer edge of a precipitous cliff. Below them was a small beach from which another track wound its way along the foreshore. A coral reef, some hundreds of yards off shore protected the beach below them from the waves which fretted in a line of foam in contrast to the still clear waters at their feet.

"Look!" said Binnie, "the water's so clear that you can see right to the bottom. I wonder if it would be safe to bathe —it's awfully hot."

Mark pondered again before replying. "I think we might ask Uncle about this—I don't think sharks would come be-yond the reef—though there is a deep-water channel—over there!"

They leaned over the edge of the cliff, lying on their stomachs to avoid giddiness.

Presently a large iguana, nearly four feet long, crawled out of the water and rested immediately below them.

"That settles bathing for me", said Mark. "It looks too much like a crocodile."

"Look! Look!" squeaked Ben. "It's a ship, quite a big one!"

Mark scanned the horizon. "I can't see anything!" he said at length.

"Not there you oaf!" said Ben, pointing down towards the reef. "Down there in the lagoon! It's a wreck !"

They all saw it. It was lying just inside the reef. Its outline was clear enough when the foam from the surf blew away for a moment. A large black vessel, totally submerged.

It was the blackness which aroused something more than passing curiosity in Mark's fertile brain. A vessel under water soon becomes festooned with weeds, slime and barnacles. This one was not so far covered in that way. Therefore it must be a very recent wreck and should be investigated.

"Let's go back and tell Uncle George", said Mark.

"And what may I ask are you going to tell Uncle George?" They turned over and looking up saw the man who called himself Tom Huntingdon, gazing benevolently at them.

"There's a wreck down there," said Mark. "We were thinking of exploring it."

Jeff Hooker had to make a quick decision and it wasn't his fault that he took the wrong one. "Oh that," he said carelessly. "That was here before I took up residence over a year ago I had a look at her myself, though it was a bit risky, what with water-snakes, sharks and lizards. Reckon whoever piled her up didn't live to tell the tale. There's a corpse in her cabin, bones as white as a hound's tooth. No place for exploring, I can tell you. Proper gruesome."

He paused while his imagination worked overtime.

"No," he went on, "you want to keep away from that bit of wreck—not healthy. When your Uncle told me where you'd gone I thought I'd follow you up and see you didn't get into trouble. What have you done to your legs, Sonny?"

"Leeches," said Mark, "I paddled in the lake."

"Did you? If you'd let me know where you was going I'd

have saved you a lot of trouble. However, we've all learned our lesson, haven't we? This is no place for young people to be let loose on. I don't know what your Uncle was thinking."

Together they went back in silence. Each of them had much on which to ponder.

Chapter Sixteen

MEANWHILE—ON "LITTLE PALMELO"

FOUR men squatted round a flat round stone. They were playing cards and were very intent on their game. Poker is played with only five cards per person; the object of the game is for each one to persuade the others that he holds the best hand. After the first deal of five cards each player may discard all or any of his hand and take fresh ones from the dealer. When this has been done the man on the left of the dealer begins to stake on his chance of winning.

In this instance it was Fatso who began the bidding, using cowrie-shells as counters, each shell representing an American dollar. Fatso had a good pile in front of him, but Tom Huntingdon had an even bigger one. It was not necessary to do more than glance at Cobbo's and Pedro's countenances to see that they were not in a winning vein.

Fatso looked at his "hand". It consisted of a pair of Jacks, a pair of Queens and a single card. Not a good one, but Poker is a game of bluff. With great confidence he said, "Five bucks." Pedro on his left hesitated. He possessed three sevens which would have beaten Fatso's hand, but how was he to know that?

With an expression of disgust he threw his cards face down. "No," he said, "dis game no good for Pedro."

Cobbo scratched his beard and tried to peep unsuccessfully at Tom Huntingdon's hand. Tom had not asked for any cards, and therefore it certainly looked as if he had been dealt with a first-class deck. On the other hand he might be bluffing, trying to frighten the others out.

Before beginning to play each man had signed a paper promising to meet his debts when civilisation was reached. Those cowrie-shells really were real money, for crooked though the three musketeers might be in many ways—they'd never have dreamed of not honouring their card-debts. People who gamble do so for the thrill of adventure. There could be no thrill if they were not playing for real money, though later on they might take second thoughts!

Cobbo looked at Tom, sitting there as cool as a cucumber; already he had become to be recognised as the leader of the marooned quartet. Tom was indeed a cool one.

"Ten", said Cobbo. He had three aces—a good hand. Tom Huntingdon's face was set in a disinterested mould.

"Fifteen", he said gently.

"Away!" said Fatso in disgust. He had decided that Tom was not bluffing and threw his cards down, pushing his five bucks into the centre of the table for the ultimate winner to collect. Now only Cobbo and Tom were "in" the game.

"Twenty", said Cobbo.

"Thirty", said Tom in a voice which suggested that he could and would keep the bidding going for ever.

Cobbo had a choice now: either to "see" his opponent, that is, to bet the same amount as Tom had and lay his cards face up when Tom would have to do the same and the best hand would then take all, or to outbid his opponent, or to throw his hand in so that Tom wouldn't discover what sort of one he'd been playing against. Which should it be? Twenty dollars was a lot of money. Should he throw good money after bad? Should he give Tom the advantage of knowing his methods? Which?

"You're a cool one", he said grudgingly—and threw his

hand in. Tom leaned forward, put his cards face down and scooped in the "money". As he did so Cobbo also leaned forward and "accidently-on-purpose" tipped Tom's deck off the "table" on the ground. They lay there face up for all to see—a valueless hand—not even a pair of deuces and Tom had frightened them all out of the game. That is Poker.

Cobbo swore mightily. "I thought you said you couldn't play Poker?" he exploded.

"I'm a fast learner", said Tom.

"You're telling me", said Fatso.

When the game was finished nearly all the shells were Tom's. He did a little sum on the back of an envelope and collected from each of his opponents an I.O.U. for the amount he was owed.

The four men were getting on famously, linked by the common bond of hostility to Jeff Hooker and, because of Tom's mysterious promise that all would be well, relieved of all anxiety. Little Palmelo was as much of a paradise as was its big brother across the water.

It had been galling to see *Rag Doll* and even more so to have to keep stoking up the bonfire without any apparent result but Tom insisted upon this. He had his methods, he said, although Jeff Hooker would probably have invented a plausible reason for ignoring the smoke signal there might be others who would not. So firm and confident did Tom appear that his suggestions soon took the form of orders. The weather held fine, the nights were a bit chilly and the mosquitoes troublesome but these were tough men, well schooled in the practice of philosophy. "Sufficient for the day is the evil thereof", was their sort of motto. Besides, they all liked this one-eyed man and a doctor to boot. Probably this period of enforced rest on Little Palmelo was the first time for many years when each of the trio had not been in fear of something. Enchantment perhaps?

Pedro had long since had his knife restored and very useful it was for the stock of provisions had consisted of canned foods and Jeff Hooker had omitted to supply a tin-opener. Without Pedro's knife their position would have been far less comfortable.

After the first twenty-four hours each man reached into his inner resources to help to make the stay tolerable. Cobbo proved to have a knowledge of basket-work, taught to him no doubt in the Reform School which he had adorned in Wogga-Wogga. There were many creepers suitable for weaving into mats and thus he made one for each of them. After that he embarked on an ambitious attempt to make an awning which would provide shade and protection against the next shower of rain. This he strung between four trees and was pleased with the plaudits of his companions.

Fatso's talents ran towards cookery, having in his day served as pantry-boy in a Chinese restaurant. With the use of empty tins as utensils he brewed up some very odd mixtures which were both warm and palatable. Pedro was the hunter. Never happy without a knife in his hand, he stalked the iguanas and seldom failed to bring one to the pot. Stripped of its scaly hide the iguana became as tender and delicate of flavour as a chicken. Frequently he cast longing glances at the great turtles but they had no cooking pot large enough to boil them in, which was fortunate for the turtles.

As for Tom, he contained his impatience and anxiety by super-human efforts and spent much of his time playing Patience with the pack of cards with which they played Poker.

So the time had passed, and life on the island which could have been a grisly affair, full of hatred and violence really deserved to be described as a picnic. Tom's fortitude and good humour inspired his fellows with confidence. Only he himself knew how thin their chances were of getting away. It all depended upon a promise made to him nearly a year ago, by a Mexican fisherman. Would he remember? If he did would he arrive in time to prevent Jeff Hooker from decamping in *Rag Doll* with all the ambergris? As he had hinted to the three musketeers it all depended upon whether Jeff would have troubled to read back through the diary he had kept since landing on the island.

And what would happen if Bernadino the fisherman had forgotten and if Jeff left them stranded?

The provisions would last a few days—after that they could exist on the natural products of the island, but—how long would these men work in harmony once they knew that they were really and truly castaways?

It was very worrying. Yet to look at him, placidly playing 'Demon' Patience, he appeared not to have a care in the world.

"Hey!" called Cobbo. "You, Fatso, don't keep shining that darned thing in my eye!"

Tom looked up. Fatso was using an empty tin as a mirror, teasing Cobbo by reflecting the sun's rays in his eye, and Cobbo was reacting accordingly.

Fatso winked at Tom and transferred the bright spot of light to Pedro who was drowsing against a boulder. Pedro sneezed and tried to brush it away. Then he woke up and grinned good-naturedly.

"Two is a better game to play than one", he declared and finding an empty tin proceeded to manœuvre himself into a position whence he could retaliate.

As he did so Tom smacked his thigh.

"Eureka!" he cried.

Chapter Seventeen

"OH WHAT A TANGLED WEB WE WEAVE——"

JEFF Hooker returned to the shack a worried man. Not over-worried, he wasn't capable of that. All his life he had lived by his wits. He told himself that he had been in tighter corners than this, but that he wouldn't succeed in his plans unless he tried a great deal harder than he had so far done.

"Oh what a tangled web we weave when first we practise to deceive"—the old quotation came to him from way back in his early days of innocence. But this would not be the first, nor indeed the twenty-first occasion on which he had "practised to deceive". The trouble with this outfit, he told himself, was that they were too jolly literal—he shied from the word "honest". He could make rings round people like Cobbo and Company, but never before in his varied life had he run across such folk as Uncle George and his merry crew. They scared him a little (not very much), especially those Green Sailors. That young shaver Ben had found the wet paint on *Black Jack*'s dinghy where Jeff had hastily covered up her name—that showed the sort of thing he, Jeff, was up against. As for the Commander, people like him always made a man nervous. Usually they were to be found in places of authority—setting on a Magistrate's bench, or standing behind the Defaulter's table. They stood for Law and Order, and Justice, with the biggest "J" in the world.

Then there was that amiable lunatic with the Canadian accent and the great bearded young man whom he had nearly mistaken for the Commander. Too much brute force there to try any violent tactics! Of course, there was always the pistol, but Jeff played his crooked games according to a set of home-made rules. He never had, and never would shoot his way out of trouble, unless it were against rival gangsters. Jeff was determined to live as long and as well as he could, and since he valued his own life dearly he had definite qualms against ending other people's. Apart from that he was prepared to go to almost any lengths, provided the reward was worth it, and surely all that ambergris—probably fifteen thousand quid's worth—was worth a great deal of effort!

The trouble was that he hadn't mugged-up the background of this blasted island! He didn't know the names of the animals, birds or reptiles—he didn't know the set-up which had sent him to live here *and* he didn't know the names of the local authorities; yet it was all there for the learning. Tom Huntingdon's papers were splashed with latin names and beautifully drawn sketches of the *fauna*; his diary was full and complete—all the information was there—only time was short. He must shut himself off from these visitors while he studied hard. Sooner or later there would be some sort of test, the wreck of the *Black Jack* would require some laughing off—and—a cold hand suddenly gripped his heart—wasn't he, Jeff, supposed to be a qualified doctor? Supposing one of these people took poorly? His own knowledge of medical matters did not go much further than the use of a hypodermic syringe to dope inconvenient meddlers, and a rough and ready remedy for alcoholic excesses.

"Jeff," he said to himself, and then corrected himself—"Tom," he said, "you got to move and move quick. Besides there's always them beggars across the water—it's a problem—a pretty problem."

He rose and after pulling the door of his shack to, dropped the venetian blinds of the windows. If people called they would be able to see that he did not wish to be disturbed.

Then, with Tom's diary and other papers in front of him he sat down to intensive study, and while he did so his fertile brain began to work out a plan for leaving the island, *with* the ambergris and *without* the crew of *Rag Doll*.

If he could get her away from her owners he could cross to Little Palmelo and embark his henchmen. Then, a coat of tar or black paint and the words *Black Jack* in substitution for *Rag Doll*, and they would be able to return to the mainland loaded with wealth. Of course Cobbo and company might act a little sore as to the way they'd been treated but he'd talk them round—he'd once sold a pair of ice-skates to a native of Central Africa, *and* in his own country. They'd soon see it his way. Yes, the way was clear and quick action was needed.

He pored over the papers, trying to memorise the names of things and people. Just fend off these inquisitive youngsters for forty-eight hours, and then Bingo!—he'd scoop a pool! It was really quite a simple problem but with these unpleasantly literal people time was valuable. Every minute he prolonged his impersonation act laid him open to detection. And with detection—he might have to use force. That wouldn't do at all. His eyes wandered to the medical cabinet where he had found the dope which had dealt so successfully with the real Tom Huntingdon. That was the best way—not messy, nor yet dangerous, but difficult to manage with three adults and four vigilant youngsters. No, it would have to be something different.

He sat for a long time and gradually the plan evolved itself. Presently it all became clear. He chuckled with delight at his own cleverness. And no one would be hurt—unless there were sharks, of course, but that, as they said in golf, was a natural hazard.

Chapter Eighteen

DANGER!

THE Trade Wind was blowing softly as the Green Sailors in *Rag Doll*'s outboard dinghy rounded the point and headed up for the weather side of the island. It had been a sudden decision to explore the sunken wreck, a decision arrived at without consulting Uncle George. They had simply borrowed the boat, leaving Tom Huntingdon's old dinghy for the use of the remainder of the crew and were feeling slightly guilty. But after examining that old dinghy whose stern had been painted over and finding traces of lettering underneath the new coat they were determined to press on regardless of risk or disapproval, for they all now suspected that there was something suspicious about their island host.

In the boat with them was a skin-diver's outfit, complete with goggles, flippers and a spring-gun belonging to Loopy. Mary had been given instructions in the use of this under-water weapon. She was to stand guard against sharks or other predatory creatures while Mark explored the interior of the wreck.

The usual loppy sea was foaming and fretting on the out-lying reef, but having seen the deep-water passage from the top of the cliff they had little difficulty in locating it when they arrived opposite the spot from which they had observed the wreck.

As a precaution, however, against hitting the rocks with the propeller of the outboard-motor Mark switched it off and lifted it into its "housed" position.

Then Mary shipped a pair of paddles and turning the dinghy's bows towards the tumbling waves backed the boat cautiously through the little channel while Binnie and Ben with grapnel and line stood by to drop anchor.

Gradually the dinghy slipped between the foam-flecked patches on either side of the channel, the occupants holding their breath in case an unsuspected bit of coral existed in the fairway and it was not until the tumbling line of water had been safely passed that anyone spoke. The Green Sailors had long since ceased to deserve their soubriquet—all they needed nowadays was luck—of pluck they had plenty.

"All right!" said Mark wiping the perspiration from his face. "We're in!"

Mary held water and then began to row parallel to the reef while Ben leaned over the bows searching for the wreck.

He soon found it. The mast which had been projecting when Cobbo had been there was now well under water, for *Black Jack* had since been lifted by the swell over the reef and now lay in deeper water inside the lagoon. Cautiously the grapnel was lowered until it caught on some part of the submerged rigging. Mary rested on her oars and allowed the little boat to drift back until the grapnel-warp came taut.

"O.K.", said Mark, as he donned his diving outfit. "Now remember, Mary, if you see any lurking monsters bang on the bailer with a rowlock under the water. I shall hear it and be on my guard. And don't fire that gun if you can avoid it. Sharks are easily frightened by noise and splashes but once blood has been drawn they will smell it for miles so we don't want to shoot until I'm out of the water and we can get away at speed. Savvy?"

Mary nodded. She was under no illusion as to the risks Mark was running and recollections of Jeff Hooker's talk of skeletons were not reassuring. How she wished that they hadn't undertaken this mission without grown-up help, but she could see that Mark had made up his mind and she wasn't going to be the one to weaken his sense of purpose.

Mark strapped the compressed-air cylinder on his back, thrust his feet into the flippers, wet the glass of his goggles before putting them on to prevent them from fogging up, adjusted them over his eyes, thrust the end of the breathing-tube into his mouth and put on the nose-clip. As he turned on the tap he felt the compressed air flowing into his lungs.

Thus equipped he clambered gingerly over the back of the dinghy—the only safe way to get out of a small boat—and paddled along until he could grasp the grapnel-warp. Then he hauled himself down into the depths below.

The water was beautifully green and clear. As he drew himself down the "exhaust" of his breathing apparatus bubbled upwards. Myriads of small tropical fish ignored him completely as they darted aimlessly about in coloured clouds. Larger and rather alarming-looking Groupers and Tunas moved out of his way. He reached the deck which was canted over nearly vertical and held himself aboard by the vessel's gunwale. One touch of the woodwork convinced him that this ship had not been under water for more than a few weeks, if that, for there was little or none of that slimy feeling which is the forerunner of weedy growth on anything which has been submerged for a longer period.

Cautiously, looking around with great trepidation he inched his way along the deck towards the stern where there was an open hatch down which he must go if he was to find out anything. The bright rays of the sun now directly over-head shone through the open skylights into the vessel's saloon. Bedding and other floatable material moved as the water surged gently through the vessel's interior, but to his great relief there was no sign of a corpse or skeleton. A million shrimps rose like a cloud of gnats on a sunny evening as he disturbed them. The sound of the surf on the reef dinned continually in his ears. So far so good.

As he looked round him Mark wondered what it was he was searching for. Some proof, perhaps of the date on which the vessel had foundered. He found the broken chart-table and eagerly reached for the notebook which lay in a crevice in it. The pages were mostly stuck together and what writing he could see was smeared and unreadable. Then he pulled on the handle of a drawer which was poised above his head while he stood on its "opposite number" on the other side of the vessel. The wood was swollen and the drawer refused to budge but he wasn't going to be so easily defeated. He hung on to the handles with both hands and allowed his feet to float up until he could brace himself for a good strong pull. Then he straightened his legs and gave a conclusive jerk. The drawer came out of its housing like a cork from a bottle and the water became filled with objects, some buoyant and others so heavy that they dropped on top of him. As he swept them out of the way he pulled the drawer towards him and examined it. A folded newspaper lay in it, stuck by its own print to the woodwork. Even as he looked at it it began to dissolve but he could see the title written in Spanish—something like "Buenaventura Tempores"—it swirled before his eyes. Eagerly he searched for the date— it should be just below the title of the paper. Yes! it was there, but—was that '1959' after the month? He had no knowledge of Spanish, the name of the month if he could have read it would have meant nothing but if he could be certain of the year of that paper it would establish when that ship had sailed from Buenaventura. Best go to the surface with the drawer before the paper disintegrated.

Then, as he moved towards the open hatch a dark shadow

passed between it and the surface and he heard the clang-clang! of the danger signal!

Looking up he fully expected to find a shark between him and safety but the shadow was the only evidence of the existence of a thing which must be by-passed before he could reach the dinghy. Cautiously he floated upwards until his head was close to the opening of the hatchway. Whilst he was inside the vessel he knew he would be safe, but his compressed air would not last for ever and before it ran out he would have to make a run for it. For a moment he felt panicky. He was trapped, unless Mary could scare the shark away, if shark it was? Better have a look.

Cautiously he put his head through the hatch—tense and ready to nip inside again if attacked. It was a daring thing to do, but anything was better than waiting without the knowledge of what was threatening him. For a moment his eyes were blinded by the strong light and he saw nothing. Then something moved quite close to him and he nearly lost his mouthpiece as he let out an involuntary yell of fear.

With the speed of light he ducked below, shaking like a jelly. He had expected to see a shark not a wizened old face with a supercilious grin on its turned-down mouth.

"You oaf!" he reproached himself, "it's only a turtle!"

He turned to look for the drawer and its contents which in his panic he had abandoned. It had floated to the roof and when examined the newspaper had disappeared in a cloud of floating particles of debris. Never mind; the condition of the woodwork, *plus* the absence of the skeleton with "bones as white as a hound's-tooth" was sufficient evidence that the man calling himself Tom Huntingdon was a first-class liar.

If Mark was happy in his relief at discovering that the

shadow which menaced him was that of a harmless turtle, Mary and her companions were not. They too had seen the great creature sunning itself as it lay idly on the surface of the lagoon and they also knew that it was harmless. That was not the reason why they had sounded the alarm. It was something far more dangerous. Binnie had just sighted it, some hundred yards distant—a large triangular black fin-shaped object which was cruising at a walking pace and approaching the wreck. It was the dorsal fin which they had learned to recognise as that of the dreaded Tiger-shark, one of the most ferocious of the species. To sit helpless in the dinghy while Mark was down below and apparently unaware of his danger was the worst ordeal the Green Sailors had so far undergone. Nervously Mary grasped the spring-gun, hoping that she would not have to pull the trigger but determined to do so if it became necessary.

"Bang that bailer again!" she ordered. Ben needed no more prompting. He leaned over the gunwale and made a tremendous clatter. The triangular fin seemed to hesitate and then turned away.

"Keep it up!" Mary's voice was croaking with anxiety, "you're frightening it away!"

Alas! She had spoken too soon. Suddenly the dorsal fin disappeared in a flurry of swirling water as the shark turned and dived in the direction of the dinghy. And as it did so the stream of bubbles which indicated Mark's position also moved in the same direction.

"He's coming up!" cried Binnie. "Oh do hurry, Mark! Do hurry up!"

Mark, of course, could hear nothing but the clanging of the bailer and the distant roar of the surf. Slightly ashamed for allowing himself to be scared by a turtle he came leisurely to the surface to show that he was not put out by these unnecessary manifestations of alarm. As he broke surface he saw Mary's strained face and Binnie's appealing looks while Ben continued to bash the bailer with all his might.

"Silly chumps!" he muttered into his mouthpiece and floated on his back while he turned off his air-supply and removed the breathing tube and nose clip. At the same moment he heard the word "shark!" and turning had a sudden glimpse of the sinister fin which had broken surface only a few yards distant. Now, fear lent both speed and strength to his actions. He kicked out with his flippers and threshed the water with his arms in every endeavour to reach the dinghy only a few feet distant, and as he did so he had the horrid knowledge that the shark could easily overtake him if it had the mind to.

Mary, white in face, raised the spring-gun and took careful aim. There was only one shot—a harpoon-shaped spear—in the gun and there would be no chance to reload. The dinghy was rocking and spoiling her aim but the situation was desperate.

"Keep still everybody!" she cried. Binnie and Ben held their breaths and froze into immobility.

"Pang!" went the spring-gun. The barbed dart flew through the air, straight for a spot a few feet short of the fin. It shot into the water and disappeared. So did the fin in a flurry. At the same moment Mark reached the dinghy's stern and grabbing the transom almost jumped out of the water. Mary flung down the gun and hauled him inboard. He lay panting for a moment while the others gazed spellbound down into the lagoon. They could see the great fish. It had started to turn over to make its attack on Mark when it had been hit in a vital part of its belly and now it was struggling in its death throes—a crimson stream of blood staining the water a delicate pink. It was the sight of this discoloration which galvanised Mark into activity. He stripped off his equipment and threw his knife to Ben.

"Cut the warp!" he ordered. "We must get out of here!"

Ben sawed away, while Mark released the outboard motor from its homed position and winding the starting cord round its fly-wheel gave a convulsive pull.

The engine started immediately and the dinghy began to move smartly ahead. Mark turned it in a wide circle and made for the entrance of the lagoon while his companions watched the spot which they had just left.

Many great fish were arriving, attracted no doubt by the smell of blood. The lagoon was being threshed into a mixture of red-foam as the hungry arrivals fastened on to the wounded shark and tore it to pieces. It was a sickening and sobering sight. When these blood-maddened beasts had devoured all there was of their victim, what next? Would they fight amongst themselves, or would they pursue the boat in their ferocious desire to assuage their whetted appetites?

Now the deep-water entrance was close ahead—once clear of the lagoon—then trouble should be over. The boat pitched into the head sea flinging clouds of spray over the occupants who saw glimpses of more and more late arrivals at the feast. Once the outboard propeller hit something and the engine faltered for a moment but it picked up again and looking astern they saw that the knife-like propeller blade had sliced another shark. Already it was having to defend itself as its companions maddened by blood-lust closed in for the kill.

Now they were in open water and pitching heavily in the on-shore sea. Mark throttled back the engine and turned in the homeward direction. It was useless to try and talk above the noise of the engine but if even it had not been no one would have spoken for they were feeling stunned by what they had just seen, and as for Mark, he knew that once again he owed his life to his sister.

She sat there white and shaken but proud that she had kept her nerve. If she had not aimed straight—it didn't bear thinking of.

Binnie and Ben cast some anxious glances behind them to see if they were being followed but soon it was clear that the sharks were only concerned in the battle which was still raging in the lagoon, and *Rag Doll* was reached without further adventures.

Chapter Nineteen

PLOT——

JEFF Hooker was in for a busy day. He returned from his private stalking of the Green Sailors more than ever convinced that time was running short. Very soon one or other of those Nosey Parkers would put him "on the spot". Confidence-tricks needed to be played fast: "the quickness of the hand deceives the eye." Likewise simple literal—he still couldn't bear to use the word "honest"—people could only be kept guessing by plenty of patter-talk. He had returned to his study of Tom Huntingdon's papers for only half an hour, however, before he heard the crunch of footsteps on the path outside. Hastily dropping the eye-shade back into position, for he found reading with two eyes hard enough going without any further handicap, he rose and went to the door of his shack.

"Welcome, Commander," he said in his benignest of manners, "come right in! You are just the man I was hoping to see."

Uncle George went in and looked around him with curiosity. He put a bundle of books on the table. "Trollope", he said. "I reckoned that a lover of Jane Austen might be glad to make his acquaintance, or is he one of your pet aversions?" Jeff, who had never heard of Anthony Trollope, or even opened a page of Miss Austen's masterpieces thanked him warmly and changed the subject.

"A friend in need is a friend indeed," he spoke as if he was coining a new phrase. "Commander," he went on, "you remember what I said in my letter to you?" He picked up the carbon copy of Tom's letter and read it out—"This much I will say—it will be worth your while to pay your old shipmate a visit, and not only for the purpose of renewing our friendship."

"Ah," said Uncle George, "that's what I came to see you about. What's the dark secret?"

Jeff hesitated for a moment before answering. He just could not get accustomed to dealing with honest people. Finally, in order to convince himself more than anything else, he said: "I know I can trust you?"

"Do you?" said Uncle George rather testily—for there was something of a query in Jeff's voice, "that's very gratifying."

"Don't get me wrong", pleaded Jeff, with a hint of desperation in his voice. "If you'd been through all what I've been through you wouldn't let your right hand trust your left."

"I understand", said Uncle George. "You wrote to me and asked me to call on you and said you wanted help. Well, here I am."

Jeff reached out and shook Uncle George's hand. "That's what I like about the Navy", he said, forcing tears into his eye to emphasise his warmth of gratitude. "I knew I could rely on you."

"Well," said Uncle George, "out with it! But I'd better warn you. If there's anything illegal about what you have to confide—I don't want to hear it. Mine is a pleasure trip, and I'm responsible for the welfare of my crew. From what I've seen of Colonel Gaspardo I should imagine that he is just panting to pop somebody into his gaol. Ever heard of a feller called Hooker?"

Jeff didn't bat an eyelid. "Sounds like a character in a

strip cartoon", he said easily. "What's he got to do with this?"

"The Colonel's on the lookout for him. He's a poacher or something—owns a ship called *Black Jack*. Has he been your way?"

Jeff had to do some quick thinking.

"There was a wreck here," he said, "sometime before I was planted here by the Christopherson Research Foundation. Four men were rescued from it and shipped home. Maybe one of them was Jeff Hooker."

He could have kicked himself as he allowed the "Jeff" to escape his lips. If Uncle George noticed the slip he said nothing.

"Well," he said, "let's have it—if it's honest."

"Honest?" exclaimed Jeff. "I know my law! Anything found below the high-water mark is legally Flotsam and Jetsam—anybody's property, and that's what I've got. Ambergris!"

"Is that all?" said Uncle George. He had been expecting pearls, at least.

"You wait," said Jeff, "there's a small fortune of the stuff. Follow me!"

He led the way down the track to the small cave whose entrance was cunningly disguised by creepers. Thrusting them aside he reached within and pulled out an iron oil drum.

"There's a dozen like this," he said pulling out a lump of the precious substance. "Three quid an ounce for the best quality stuff. And there's close on 300 pounds dead weight in that cave. Call it fifteen thousand quid's worth and we won't quarrel about it!"

Uncle George took a lump and sniffed at it.

"Yes," he said, "this is the real stuff all right. Now, where do *I* come in?"

"I want you to have it—not all of it, of course, but if you'll ship it aboard your yacht and take it where you can dispose of it at the right price you can have ten-per-cent of the proceeds. That fair enough?"

"You want me to ship it out of here, is that it?"

"Sure, Commander. It's the only chance—those beggars over at San Cristobal would scoff the lot if they knew about it. Legal, or not legal."

"What about you?" asked Uncle George—"I can't take you with the ambergris—I've no room for passengers."

"That's what I keep saying", said Jeff earnestly. "I can *trust* you. I'll stay here until my time's up. You can flog this lot and put the proceeds in your bank until you hear from me. How about it?"

That was certainly an open-handed offer. There seemed to be no snag about it. Wild horses wouldn't have succeeded in making Uncle George take Jeff Hooker along with him. Whether he was the original Tom Huntingdon or not—he wouldn't have fitted aboard *Rag Doll*—but his offer seemed to be fair enough: ten-per-cent of fifteen thousand pounds! Not to be sneezed at.

Jeff had baited the trap well. "Very well", said Uncle George. "I will do what you wish. Better ship the stuff aboard as soon as you can, in case we have unwelcome visitors. According to Colonel Gaspardo—this—er—Jeff Hooker feller may be along any time now. You did say his name was Jeff, didn't you?"

"Did I?" Jeff grinned, "telepathy's my middle name."

"The man's a crook," thought Uncle George, "but quite an engaging one. And he's paid me the greatest compliment in the world—to entrust all that wealth to my keeping." One couldn't help feeling friendly towards him.

"I'll hail Ted and Loopy," he said briskly, "you launch

your motor-boat and we'll load it up—no time like the present!"

He went quickly down the hill. Jeff watched him with a sympathetic smile. Poor old Codger—he'd fallen for it all right. It was a shame to take the money but—well—this world they lived in was nothing but a rat-race. Mugs like the Commander deserved what was coming to them.

Once the stuff was aboard the ketch the rest would be easy. And the sooner the quicker!

Chapter Twenty

—AND COUNTER-PLOT!

THE four Green Sailors arrived back alongside *Rag Doll* to find a scene of great activity. The motor-boat belonging to Tom Huntingdon had been launched and loaded with ambergris which was now being discharged into the yacht's capacious bilges.

So busy were the adults that Mark, Mary, Binnie and Ben had little opportunity to voice their suspicions of the *bona fides* of the owner of the treasure.

They managed, however, to tell Loopy quite a lot about their adventures. For once he listened carefully and seriously while Mark explained the state of the wreck of *Black Jack* and his doubts of the story that she had been there over a year. Loopy had taken an instinctive dislike for Jeff Hooker and was still smarting under a snub which Uncle George had administered when he, Loopy, had advised him to have nothing to do with the ambergris.

"When you have lived as long as I have, my friend," Uncle George had said, "you will realise that possession is nine points of the law. Now get cracking and stow this stuff aboard."

"The old boy's carried away by the sight of all this wealth —I guess", he whispered to the Greens. "He'll land us all in trouble, or I'm a Dutchman. Reckon it's time to have a showdown."

"But how?" asked Mary.

Loopy looked very cunning. "Perhaps you don't remember

that I studied medicine for over two years," he said, "before I came into my money. You can learn a whale of a lot of technical talk in two years. Guess it's time I tried it on *Doctor* Huntingdon. What's the matter with your legs, Mark?"

Mark told him about the leeches. "Fine, fine!" said Loopy. "Guess you need medical attention—I'll slip ashore and organise the 'Doctor'!"

With a broad wink, he dropped lightly into the dinghy and set off ashore.

He made his way up to the shack and waited there for Jeff to return, and whilst there he took the opportunity of consulting a dictionary. By the time Jeff's footsteps could be heard as he returned after hauling up the motor-boat Loopy was ready with his trap.

Half an hour later he returned to *Rag Doll* just as light was failing. As he entered the saloon he became aware immediately of an atmosphere of grave concern.

Uncle George had now heard Mark's account of the affair of the wreck and the encounter with the sharks. He was angry with the Greens for taking the risks they had and had said so in good round terms. He wasn't, he said, such an old fool as they thought. He said he had had suspicions of the man since he had first met him, but suspicion wasn't enough. If, as they supposed, this man was not the real Tom Huntingdon, query—who was he, and where was Tom?

At this stage Loopy had arrived. "I can tell you what he isn't, Commander," he said, "he's no doctor. I just played a simple joke on him and this is how it went—I said to him—'Doc, I'm worried about young Mark Green—he's had a lot of trouble with his Mediastinum.' That for the information of all those ignorant of medical science, ladies and gentlemen, is the cavity between the lungs. Any first year medical student must begin by learning such an elementary bit of anatomy. Even I know that—but the 'Doc'—I could see hadn't a clue. 'Mediastinum', he said, stroking his chin. 'Mediastinum?' 'Yes,' I said, 'his *legs* are in a terrible state. It's been in the family for years.'

"'Ah,' he says, 'when it's like that it's best to let nature take its course. Time,' he says, 'is a great healer.'

"That seemed pretty definite to me, but I thought I'd go one further, so I told him that I'd had a talk with a specialist about Mark's condition and he'd advised that if the trouble came on again to tell the nearest doctor that a 'Sesamoid Macropus' frequently did the trick. Failing that, I said, he had advised a solution of a mixture of 'Matuta and Macrura', applied hourly, but if that didn't work the chances were that 'Lyssa' would set in.

"Well, he swallowed it all, nodding wisely as if what I'd quoted to him made sense."

"What did it mean?" asked Ted.

"Sesamoid," explained Loopy, "is an adjective appertaining to the seed 'sesame'. 'Macropus' is another word for Kangaroo."

"'Matuta' I know was the ancient Roman Goddess of creation," said Ted grinning broadly, "but what in the world are or is 'Macrura'?"

"Shrimps and Lobsters," said Loopy; "and 'Lyssa'," he added, "is another word for 'Rabies'."

Uncle George slammed the table with his hand.

"Well done, Loopy!" he said. "That's the proof that this man is not the Tom Huntingdon that I knew all those years back. Now the problem is what to do next?"

He looked at the eager faces round the table.

Mary was the first to speak. She went to the point which was worrying them all. "Do you think," she asked, "that this man has——" she hesitated and Loopy supplied the word she baulked at.

"—bumped off," he prompted.

"—bumped off the genuine Tom Huntingdon?"

"What do you think, Loopy?" asked Uncle George.

"I'd say, 'no'", said Loopy. "I'd say that he's not that sort of a guy."

"Then what do you think has happened?" asked Mary.

"I think that this feller is one of the crew of the ship-wrecked *Black Jack*—probably Jeff Hooker himself", said Uncle George gravely. "I don't share your opinion as to his innocent intentions, Loopy."

"But what has happened to the rest of the crew?" asked Mark.

"Find them and you'll probably find the real Tom Hunt-ingdon", said Ted. Suddenly he slapped his knee—"I've got it!" he said.

"So have I—I think," said Uncle George, "and to-morrow I'll try and prove my theory. Did you persuade the 'Doc', as you call him, Loopy, to come and visit this young gentleman who is suffering from Rabies?"

"Sure", said Loopy. "I did that and I took the pre-caution of doing away with his dictionary before he turned up—just in case he looked those long words up. I guess he'll come along tomorrow morning and prescribe a dose of sesamoid shrimps."

Mark grinned.

"Well," said Uncle George, "while he's examining the patient I want to have a good look round his shack. If he was the owner of *Black Jack* he'd be certain to have rescued his ship's papers—a skipper of any vessel will do that, almost by instinct. If I can find *Black Jack*'s papers among his possessions I shall know what to do. Put the whole matter

before Colonel Gaspardo and institute a search for the miss-
ing members of the crew and Tom Huntingdon. Until
tomorrow then, ladies and gentlemen, the meeting is
adjourned."

Down on the foreshore a figure moved silently. Jeff
Hooker was also making plans for the morrow and was
taking the precaution of putting the motor-boat out of
action. With a brace and bit he bored a dozen holes in her
hull and removing the magneto from the engine hid it under
some loose rocks. This would ensure that nothing would
interfere with his chosen method of taking possession of *Rag
Doll*. The invitation to visit the sick boy aboard the yacht
was just what he had wanted. With any luck he would gain
possession of her without recourse to violence—but if that
was not possible there was always the pistol.

Pity if he had to use it, he liked doing these things by
sheer cunning—he slept better at nights that way.

"Jeff," he said to himself, "you're about to pull off the
coup of the century—bless them all!"

Chapter Twenty-One

OPERATION "EUREKA"

TOM HUNTINGDON awoke with the first light of dawn. He went at once to look across the strait to see if *Rag Doll* was still there. To his great relief he could see that she was.

He returned to the camp where Cobbo, Pedro and Fatso were snoring in close harmony, looking in their sleep like hairy-faced babies, free from things which trouble the conscience, and completely relaxed.

It seemed a pity to disturb them, but time was everything, so he banged a tin can until they sat up rubbing their eyes and demanded to know what was eating him.

He told them. The task he had set himself and them was not yet completed. In trying to produce a mirror large enough to reflect the sun's rays far enough to attract the attention of those aboard *Rag Doll* Tom Huntingdon had run across a lot of difficulties, but he throve on such snags. He had a natural gift for making gadgets which worked and when he had cried "*Eureka*"—which everybody knows is an exclamation which people use when they are delighted in finding that for which they are seeking—he had hit upon a method of signalling by means of what is scientifically called a Heliograph. This usually consists of a horizontal mirror which reflects the sun's rays on to another mirror which can be tilted so that an observer at a distance such as somebody in *Rag Doll* would see intermittent spots of light which could be spaced to represent the "shorts" and "longs" of the Morse Code. It was a simple enough device, but with the resources at his disposal the problem of constructing it was considerable. For reflecting surfaces there were plenty of tin cans: these had to be cut up, beaten flat and polished with coral sand until they gleamed like burnished armour. In order to throw a beam of light five miles across the strait a curved or concave mirror must be constructed and it must be at least twelve inches in diameter. Here Tom's luck stood him in good stead. Cobbo produced two turtle-shells—the cast-off property of dead Galapagoes and having almost the exact amount of curvature required for a concave mirror though not completely round. With the aid of a mixture of clay and sand Tom had lined the interior of one shell until it was a perfectly-shaped concave and a steady enough base on which to fix the "mirror".

The worst problem had been to join the pieces of polished tin together and then cut it into the right shape to fit inside the concave shell. All the day before Pedro and Cobbo had pounded and cut at the material. They had tried to produce one slightly dented disc, but in vain. Then Tom had the idea of making it from four quadrantal pieces which fitted together at the centre of the circle. When these had been pounded into shape they were laid inside the concave shell and sewn in position with needle and twine which Tom had purchased at San Cristobal and which had been pitched ashore with the rest of the stores. It was a most ingenious bit of work, and when presented to the direct rays of the sun was powerful enough to act as a burning-glass at the focal point of the mirror. The next thing to do was to mount the entire contraption on trunnions so that it could be tilted in a vertical plane and so throw its beam either directly at *Rag Doll* or slightly above her mast. This presented no great difficulty. Two holes were bored in the shell—two wooden pegs were driven into the holes and the whole affair was then balanced on two forked sticks driven into the ground. Thus the tilting mirror was completed. The horizontal reflector whose duty was to catch the sun's rays was an easier job, for it did not have to be a curved surface but it took a long time to hammer a sheet of tin so that it was completely flat, and then to lay it so that it was horizontal. This was at last achieved by using the other Galapago's shell as a sort of spirit-level. It was laid on the ground in a specially prepared shallow hole and three-quarters filled with water. Then marks were made on the interior of the shell where the surface of the water touched it all round. The water was then bailed out of the shell and sand was substituted up to the same level, using the marks as guides. Then the mirror was laid on the surface of the sand and Tom knew that he had a completely flat and horizontal surface.

By the time all that had been done the sun had set, and it had not been possible to test the apparatus. So they had eaten from their fast-diminishing stock of tins, and had slept through the darkness.

With daylight the work was recommenced, and as the sun rose steeply out of the eastern horizon Tom began to make his adjustments. There would be about half-an-hour when the direction of the sun's rays would be suitable for reflecting them in *Rag Doll*—was as long as a fixed contraption could be used. It might be possible after that to use the mirror by hand, but not to make morse-code signals.

Cobbo, Fatso and Pedro were enormously impressed by Tom's ingenuity. To have made a heliograph out of tins of Baked Beans and a couple of old turtle-shells was, to quote Cobbo—"a flaming miracle".

While they waited for the most favourable moment to start the signalling Tom amused himself by fixing a handle to the tilting mirror as well as a couple of stops to prevent it

Tom Huntingdon's Morse Heliograph. The upper reflecting line would be invisible to Rag Doll, making the "dark" intervals of each Morse letter.

from moving too far. By the time he had completed it it looked a throughly professional job.

There was one cigarette left between the lot of them. They tossed for it and Tom of course won. As he smoked it they watched the long shadow of a palm tree shortening and moving as the sun climbed in the heavens until it was directly behind the distant yacht. Then Tom rose, and going to the apparatus began to flash his signal. "S.O.S.— S.O.S—S.O.S" Over and over again. Whether the light was reaching as far as *Rag Doll*, or was directed accurately enough to be seen and read—only time could tell.

After the S.O.S. series he went on to pass a message. "Beware," he flashed: "of man calling himself Tom Huntingdon! Come at once! Beware of Tom Huntingdon."

Click! Click! went the swinging mirror.

"Flamin' marvellous!" said Cobbo.

"All done by mirrors!" added Fatso.

"Magnifico," said Pedro, "but does it succeed?"

He craned his eyes into the sunlit path which joined the distant yacht to Little Palmelo Island.

Steadily Tom operated his contraption and as he did so the shadow of the palm tree moved further round until with a final flourish of "S.O.S's" he abandoned the thing.

"That's all for today," he said. "Tomorrow we'll do it again—if she's still there."

They felt curiously depressed. So much effort had been made and there was no means of telling whether it had succeeded!

Pedro continued to watch the yacht which was now more clearly visible. Suddenly he let out an oath—"Caramba! she is coming—she is coming!" His voice rose to a squeak. He turned and threw his arms round Tom kissing him on either cheek. "Mister Tom—Mister Tom—everything I have not already lost to you at poker is yours!"

Cobbo slapped him on the back and shouted, "Bonzer!" several times, while Fatso executed a curious mixture of Jive and Hornpipe. There was no doubt about it. Tom Huntingdon was a very popular man at that moment.

Meanwhile the yacht came steadily nearer.

Chapter Twenty-Two

"THE BEST LAID PLANS O' MICE AND MEN GANG AFT A-GLEY."

Robert Burns.

JEFF Hooker was awake as early as the man who he was pretending to be. His pulses quickened with pleasurable anticipation of the adventures which lay ahead of him. All his life he had gloried in the moments of action which brought him gains. Today promised to be the best ever.

After Loopy's departure Jeff, who was not as green as the young Canadian had thought him to be, searched for his dictionary and when he had found it concealed under an old mat on the patio his suspicions were aroused. He couldn't remember all the Latin names which Loopy had so glibly quoted but one had remained in his mind. It was "Macropus" and according to the dictionary that meant Kangaroo! "So," thought Jeff, "that young Canuck has been taking the micky out of me; well, he'll live to regret it."

At the appointed hour Jeff walked down to the beach and as he did so *Rag Doll's* dinghy rowed by Loopy and containing Uncle George and Ted, put off from the yacht and came to the landing-place. Jeff greeted them blandly and listened to Uncle George's explanation that he and Ted were going for a ramble as if he believed them. "What a turn up for the book!" he said to himself. "With them two out of the way it'll be a piece of cake!"

When the two explorers had departed Loopy beckoned Jeff to get into the dinghy but that didn't suit Jeff at all.

159

So he said that he liked to be independent and would use his own boat, thus ensuring that Uncle George and Ted were well and truly marooned.

Meanwhile Mark, trying to look like a sick patient, had fixed himself up with a few cushions in the cockpit while Mary was giving last-minute instructions to the younger members of the family not to giggle or look suspicious.

The two dinghies arrived alongside *Rag Doll* almost simultaneously. Jeff with a broad grin, moored his up and gave Loopy a helping hand.

"So this is the patient," he said as he saw the recumbent figure stretched out on the cockpit seat. "Let's have a look at him." Removing the Elastoplast from the small incisions which the leeches had made, he cocked his head on one side and dwelt a pause. At last the waiting Greens heard his verdict.

"He'll live," he said, "Kangaroo fever or Rabies—it's all the same." He turned to the disconcerted Loopy and said with a smile: "You did well but not well enough, Mister. Maybe you thought I wasn't a real doctor?"

Loopy didn't know what to say to this unexpected attack. He just gaped. Jeff laughed genially. "You were not so far wrong", he said. "I reckon I've pretty well forgotten most of my medical training. If your Commander Firebrace has such a thing as a manual of medicine aboard maybe you'd allow me to stay awhile and refresh my memory?"

Such frankness was disarming. All aboard were feeling foolish. Jeff had them at a disadvantage. He had at last discovered the right way to outwit honest people, by being honest himself.

Mary gave Loopy a look of reproach before answering Jeff. "If you'd like to come below," she said, "I'll get you the book. It'll be quieter there if you want to read."

He thanked her and followed her below to the saloon where she produced Uncle George's *Manual of First Aid*, made him a cup of coffee and tiptoed away.

As soon as she was gone Jeff cautiously explored the interior of the yacht. There were certain things he must find out before he put his plan into action. He must know how to start the engine and how the anchor was weighed. When the moment came to act he must act quickly.

The engine was forward in *Rag Doll* and so he was able stealthily to lift the top cover and to search for the fuel-cocks. Before, however, he had time to give more than a quick glance he heard footsteps and turning saw Binnie looking hard at him.

"Hullo, young lady!" he said.

"Hullo", said Binnie. "What are you doing?"

A straight question deserved an equally straight answer. "Looking at your engine. What sort is it?"

"It's a diesel," said Binnie, "why do you want to know?"

"Natural curiosity", said Jeff. "You're curious, too, aren't you?" he added.

"Sometimes", said Binnie.

"Not mechanically minded?"

"I don't know what that means."

"I mean I bet you don't know how to start this engine."

"How much?" Binnie's eyes sparkled.

"Five bucks?"

"What's a buck?" asked Binnie.

"American dollar—five bucks is the best part of two quid, English. How about a little bet, eh?"

Binnie shook her head. "Uncle George says it's wrong to bet on certainties", she said. "You see I've started this engine dozens of times. It wouldn't be fair to take your money."

L

161

"That's one way of covering up your ignorance", said Jeff coolly, picking up his medical book as if to dismiss the whole subject.

"You shouldn't say that," said Binnie, "it isn't fair."

"Run away, there's a good child", said Jeff contemptuously. "I've something better to do than to talk to little girls who tell fibs and pretend they know things that they don't."

Binnie stamped her foot with rage.

"I do know how to start the engine!" she cried passionately, "so there!"

"All right, prove it and you shall have your five bucks."

If Binnie had not been stung into resentment by his suggestion that she was ignorant she would have remembered her suspicions and kept her mouth shut. As it was she was filled with determination to prove to this sneering visitor that she was not an ignorant little girl. And so she told him all about the engine—the anchor and how the winch was worked by hydraulic pressure, and Jeff pretending to take no interest absorbed every detail.

On deck the others were talking in low voices. Mark was definitely resentful. "The trouble with everybody in this packet," he said, "is that they are too jolly suspicious and try to be too jolly clever."

"O.K." said Loopy, "is my face red, or is it red?"

"If you ask me," said Mark, "it's as much Uncle's fault as any one's. Fancy not remembering what an old shipmate of his looks like!"

Mary tried to pour oil on the troubled waters. "I think we've all got bees in our bonnets", she said. "When Uncle George comes back I'm going to ask him to take us somewhere else—all this suspicious talk is spoiling everything."

"Hear hear!" said Mark. He stirred restlessly and sat up. "Oh for a swim!" he cried. "I wonder if there are sharks as close in shore as this?"

Ben clambered up the ratlines on the shrouds until he had reached the lower cross-trees. It was his favourite trick to do this. Once up there he balanced himself on the horizontal spar which formed the cross-tree, and shading his eyes peered into the translucent depths of the sea.

"I can see the bottom," he called, "and there isn't a fish in sight!"

Mary looked nervously at Mark. "You're not to go in, Mark!" she said: "Uncle George said——"

"Just in and out," suggested Mark, "with Ben watching from aloft there wouldn't be any risk." He began to strip off.

"Hi!" shouted Ben. "There's something flashing over on the other island. Look!"

They all turned and saw it at once. It shone like a wind-screen of a motor-car when it reflects the sun's rays and it differed in one way only. The dazzling light kept switching off and on as if worked deliberately to do this. Shading his eyes Mark, whose Morse Code was first-class, began automatically to count the short flashes and the long ones and soon began to read the signals.

"Somebody's signalling," he said.

Ben came whizzing down the main halyard to join the group. "Write it down, somebody!" called Mark. In his excitement he had raised his voice and this was to prove the undoing of *Rag Doll*'s crew.

"—S.O.S. Beware—" The words came down the open hatchway where Jeff was still busily jollying information out of Binnie.

With a quick panther-like movement he went up the

Mark went next, followed by Mary.

companionway to the deck-house, a silent and menacing figure. No one in the cockpit saw him until it was too late. He tackled Loopy first, butting him violently in the stomach before picking him up and hurling him over the side. Mark went next, followed by Mary. Ben started to run forward but Jeff was on him before he had time to move.

"Can you swim, sonny?" Jeff's better nature was making him careful.

"Of course I can!" said Ben.

"Then enjoy yourself!" said Jeff picking him up and throwing him overboard.

At the sound of the splashings Binnie came running up. After being asked the same question she too joined the others. Jeff went quickly to where his dinghy was moored and cast it off.

"Better get into the boat," he called, "we don't want any accident with sharks!" Then he picked up a boat-hook and waved it. "And don't try coming back onboard", he snarled as viciously as he could manage. "Give my respects to the Commander!"

He bent down and pressed the self-starter button which Binnie had so obligingly described to him. The engine sprang to life. Nimbly he ran forward and pushed the lever of the hydraulic winch over to "Heave in".

Up came the cable. Then, when the anchor was in sight Jeff nipped aft and flung the gear-lever to "ahead". *Rag Doll* gathered way and turned seaward. Jeff steadied her up and turning, saw with satisfaction that all five members of the crew were now in the dinghy.

"No bones broken", he muttered. "So far so good!"

Chapter Twenty-three

MAROONED! (II)

THIS was undoubtedly the worst thing that had ever happened to Uncle George and his far-from-merry crew.

During the times they had spent aboard *Rag Doll* and her predecessor of the same name, they had been face-to-face with many kinds of dangerous situations, all of which aroused in them a fierce determination to fight for victory, which resolution had always brought them through to ultimate triumph over adversity. But how could you fight against such a misfortune as theft? There is something soul-sickening at the discovery of any sort of loss due to thieves. The thing that was there has gone—one is face-to-face with nothing. And the indignity of it! To be inveigled ashore, as Uncle George and Ted had been: to be literally chucked off the yacht, as the rest of the crew had been: both were shameful experiences—not the sort of story to tell one's friends. And there was the awful feeling that Jeff Hooker would not know, or even care whether he knew how to look after the good ship which had brought them through tempest and tribulations to this ill-starred island which they all were beginning to hate.

As soon as Uncle George had seen what had happened he had raced down to the shore, not to hear the woeful story of the piracy of his craft and how it had been accomplished—but to take positive action to recover her. Straight for the motor-boat he went, and in his haste he did not look to see if she was sea-worthy. Releasing the brake on the winch he

allowed her to slide swiftly into the sea with Ted aboard her
to disconnect the tackle. It was another case of the final
straw which broke the camel's back when she filled up and
sank as soon as she was water-borne. Jeff Hooker had laid
his plans well—they were all truly marooned!

Sadly the whole party wended its disconsolate way back
to the shack. Binnie was in tears and Ben not far off them
for he kept wondering what would happen to Polly. Mary
was white-faced and angry, and Mark, who had pooh-
poohed all the talk of suspicion, silent and ashamed. Loopy
was voluble and apologetic. Ted clenched his fists in futile
resolution to knock Jeff Hooker's "block" off.

Uncle George turned his attention to taking stock of the
resources at his disposal. There was a fair amount of tinned
food, plenty of water and lots of available game and fish for
the killing. They would be all right until rescue in the form
of Colonel Gaspardo's patrol-boat came along; in fact they
would be much too comfortable. What the blazes were they
to do to pass the time? And how very foolish they would
appear when the story became public property!

The sight of the woebegone faces of his young crew reminded him of his duty as captain. He must cheer his
people up, and what was more important, arrange for a
round-the-clock look-out during daylight hours to be estab-
lished with a big bonfire ready to be touched off if any vessel
was sighted. Piracy-on-the-High-Seas is a very serious
crime—the perpetrator automatically becomes an interna-
tional outlaw; all vessels would therefore immediately assist
by every means in their power to apprehend the miscreants.
In these days of radio Jeff Hooker would be lucky if he
escaped completely, *provided* that the word went out soon.
Give him a week or ten days, however, to shift himself a
thousand miles away and to disguise the vessel and he might

167

get clean away. Of course *Rag Doll* was heavily insured, and that was some sort of comfort, but the thought of being out-witted by such a ruffian as Jeff Hooker rankled.

The main thing to do was to keep everybody busy. The shack was small and not meant to accomodate more than one or two people. They were seven. So Mary was told to try and fix up beds for all. There was quite a store of canvas and rope. Uncle George demonstrated how to make one hammock and left Mary and Ted to get busy with the re-mainder.

Mark and his two juniors were sent off with the sledge to cut down fire-wood and to tow it to the highest point of the island where Loopy was already posted as Look-out.

Uncle George went back to the scene of the sunken motor-boat to which he swam out, and diving examined the hull. He soon discovered the cause of the leaks and reckoned that if they were stopped the boat might be got going, not as a motor-boat for he could also see that the magneto was mis-sing and had already discovered that Jeff had poured all the petrol away, but with a little ingenuity he might fix up a mast and make a sail. Then he would consider the possibility of sailing the twenty miles to San Cristobal though such a trip to windward would not be easy to acomplish.

By nightfall a big bonfire had been erected and the make-shift hammocks had been slung. A meal of cocoa and bis-cuits was taken, and then, exhausted both physically and mentally, they all turned in except Uncle George who stated that he would be the first look-out when dawn broke; as they got into their hammocks he bade them be of good cheer.

"I have a feeling," he said, "that all will be well." It was a brave saying and spoken with conviction. The Greens took comfort from the apparent serenity of their Leader and very soon the little shack was filled with the sound of heavy breathing as one after the other fell asleep.

Only Uncle George remained awake. His mind teemed with ideas and half-made plans against any possible eventuality. Like all good thinkers he put himself in the place of Jeff Hooker. What would that gentleman do? Pick up the remainder of his crew, no doubt. Who had been responsible for flashing the S.O.S.? Did that mean that Tom Huntingdon was both alive and free to call for help? Supposing that Jeff Hooker was an even greater scoundrel than he had so far appeared to be—a man who would stick at nothing—what would he do to protect himself against possible detection in the future? An ugly thought came to Uncle George's mind. Dead men (or for that matter—girls and boys) tell no tales. Might not *Rag Doll* reappear with a crew of desperados who would make it their business to eliminate all traces of the original owners before disguising the ketch as their own boat *Black Jack?* If Jeff Hooker was completely ruthless that would be his safest course of action. Having committed piracy it was only a step further to murder!

As the night crawled on Uncle George formulated a plan to defeat any possible invasion. If Jeff Hooker did decide to return to the island for the fell purpose of disposing of them all, they must be ready for him and his companions. Supposing there were four of the scoundrels—all grown men—the *Rag Doll*'s party outnumbered them by three. Three adults —plus Mark who was a lusty chap—call it four against four plus Mary, Binnie and Ben who could be very useful at long range. His mind seething with plans Uncle George tiptoed out of the shack and reconnoitred the ground where if he had to he would fight the battle.

There was a moon, a clear sky and the air was heavy

with scent and the sound of innumerable insect-wings. The distant roar of the surf was strangely muted as if the night was holding its breath.

Climbing to a mound which overlooked the track between the beach and the shack Uncle George stood thinking. If he placed his young Greens there and armed them with stones which they could lob on to the heads of the people below it would create the necessary diversion while the four of them attacked from the shelter of the undergrowth. A perfect ambush with the great advantage of complete surprise. Shading his eyes into the silvery reflection of the moon's rays he searched carefully for any signs of an approaching vessel, but saw and heard nothing. By now he was so obsessed with his idea of a surprise attack by Jeff Hooker and his myrmidons that he decided to stay out and keep watch. At midnight he would rouse Ted and let him take on. They definitely must not be caught napping!

He squatted on a convenient hummock, feeling the gentle breeze fanning his face. Bright though the moon might be it seemed unlikely that Jeff Hooker, who had already wrecked one ship would risk doing so again. Perhaps, thought Uncle George, I'm making too much of the whole affair; perhaps Hooker was only a common sneak and no murderer, but what about the others?

Steadily the night wore on and as it did so the moon sank into the sea and it became dark. Now there was no further danger until daylight. He went back to the shack and stretched himself out on Tom Huntingdon's bed.

The first rays of light found him out and about again. Quickly he climbed to the high point and searched the horizon. Nothing there! Then he looked down at the cove where *Rag Doll* had lain and as he did so he caught his breath with astonishment. *There she was*, at anchor! Was it a mirage? No. There were men on her deck. Four of them. They were doing something to the boat. They were coming ashore. There was no time to be lost. Uncle George turned and ran for his life and the lives of his companions.

Chapter Twenty-Four

THE FIGHT

WITH beating hearts three Greens crouched in their appointed position on top of the mound at the bottom of
which lay the track. Down in the undergrowth which verged
on the little path the four others were waiting. Each was carrying a short weapon made by sawing broomsticks in half. The
main object of the attackers, Uncle George explained, must
be to neutralise any firearms which the invaders might be
carrying. A sharp crack across the wrist of any man who was
holding a weapon would cause him to drop it. Once the
risk of shooting had been eliminated—the battle was to be
fought in retreat, thus leading the invaders away from their
landing place. At this stage the three Green Sailors were to
nip down to the shore and go onboard *Rag Doll*. If Uncle
George and his people did not reappear within an hour or so
they were to up-anchor and make for San Cristobal at full
speed, there to raise the alarm. It was a beautifuly worked-
out plan which would only have failed if the invaders had
left one of their number aboard.

Loopy who had climbed a tree to spy on the enemy reported however that all four men had got into the dinghy and
were at that very moment pulling for the shore.

Uncle George called softly to Mary. "Stand by there!
And don't make a sound until I blow my whistle. Have you
plenty of stones?"

"Oodles", called back Mary.

"Good! Now lie quiet and wait!"

Easy to say, but hard to do. Every soldier knows what an agony it is, waiting for zero hour. Mary lay on her stomach and held Binnie and Ben by each hand. Far below her she heard the keel of the dinghy grating on the shingle as it touched the shore, then she heard the sound of the boat being pulled up above high water and then the heavy crunch of boots as the enemy began to ascend the steep little track.

"They're coming!" whispered Binnie.

"Hush!" whispered Mary, though it was really quite unnecessary for the invaders were making so much noise that it drowned all else. They were talking a little and swearing a lot as they slipped and slithered on the rough track. It was curious that they had neglected to effect a surprise attack, but no doubt they were supremely confident of their ability to succeed in their object, whatever it might be. That, to Uncle George, meant firearms for sure. This was going to be a desperate affair.

As the footsteps and voices came nearer Mark had an irresistible desire to sneeze. Loopy, lying next to him pulled a piece of well-chewed gum out of his mouth and stuck it into Mark's. "That'll stop it", he whispered. He was right. It did. Uncle George fingered his whistle examining it carefully to make certain that it was not choked with fluff or sand. Up on the top of the mound Mary, Binnie and Ben raised themselves to a standing position, each with a hefty rock in hand.

Steadily the voices came nearer. Loud, uncouth and rather frightening voices—swaggering triumphant voices—piratical voices. One of them said: "It'll damned well serve him right."

Another said: "You should allow me to use the knife."

Another said: "I'm looking forward to meeting up with this Commander Firebrace—I knew a cobber of that name back in Sidney."

Then the footsteps ceased and a voice said, "Gee, I'm out of condition. Where's the hurry? I'd give my back teeth for a smoke."

"Then let's get cracking", said another. "There'll be plenty where we're going."

The footsteps were resumed. Now the Greens could hear the heavy breathing of the man who proclaimed his unfitness to the world. Uncle George's hopes ran high, a good punch in the belly would deal with him—that made only three. He raised his whistle to his lips and motioned to his companions to stand by.

"I wonder if there's any more of that alcohol left—it sure packed a wallop", said a voice.

Peering out of the greenery Uncle George saw them. Four men, one with a black patch over his eye—the leader of the gang and the cause of all this trouble. The others were a hairy, dirty lot of scoundrels: one was so fat that he could hardly move—another carried a knife in his belt, and the third looked a very ugly customer. They were taking it easy as they steadily climbed; there seemed to be no particular urgency in their movements, supremely confident as they were, no doubt, in the outcome of their mission. In such a manner had the Spanish Armada swaggered up the English Channel, until it had encountered the opposition.

Uncle George blew a prodigious blast which at once brought the four men to a surprised standstill. At the same moment a shower of stones came down from above, causing the men to duck and dodge.

"What the flaming——" a sharp stone had caught Cobbo a crack on his head.

"Come on!" roared Uncle George. "At 'em! Beat 'em up!"

All four rose from their ambush and came down on the

invaders, whirling their batons and striking in all directions. Uncle George made for the man with the black patch over his eye. "Take that!" he growled as he swung his stick above his head. Fatso was already down but Pedro had drawn his knife.

"Hold it!" The man with the black patch stood motionless as he uttered his warning in a voice which was certainly *not* that of Jeff Hooker. "My dear Firebrace," he went on in the broadest of Scots accents—"we're on your side. I'm Tom Huntingdon and these are my very good friends!"

"Cease fire!" yelled Uncle George.

Chapter Twenty-Five

WHAT A SURPRISE FOR JEFF HOOKER!

FOUR men stood in a little group at the water's edge, watching Jeff Hooker as he let go *Rag Doll*'s anchor and hauled the dinghy alongside, preparatory to rowing himself ashore. Each man was too preoccupied with his thoughts to speak, for none had expected to see Jeff Hooker aboard the yacht.

Tom Huntingdon had a momentary impulse to make a dash for it away on to the high land. Here was he, one man against four—four that is, if Cobbo, Fatso and Pedro resumed their allegiance to Hooker—of that he couldn't be sure, for there was something coldly menacing about the attitude of the "three musketeers" as they watched the approach of their erstwhile skipper, who had marooned them. How would they react? He didn't have long to wait. Cobbo turned to him and said: "Not to worry, Mister. You leave this to us."

Jeff began to speak as soon as he came within earshot. He knew he'd have to talk fast—he had ditched his companions and would have to explain why before anyone got wrong ideas. As for Huntingdon—he was hopelessly outnumbered so there was no need to worry about him.

"Hi!" he called. "I've got the lot! The boat—the ambergris and the ruddy parrot!"

He backed one paddle and propelled the dinghy stern-first towards the water's edge.

"You don't look very pleased to see me," he went on,

"don't you understand? Fifteen thousand quid's worth of ambergris—and that yacht. We're in the money!"

Still a stony silence from the three men.

As the dinghy's stern grated on the sand Cobbo leaned forward and hauled it high and dry while Fasto, attended by Pedro—with his knife—seized Jeff and removed his pistol.

"Hey!" he protested, "that's no way to treat a pal!"

"Pal nothing," said Cobbo, "what have you done with the people whose boat that is?"

Jeff roared with laughter. "You don't think I've hurt 'em do you? Me, as wouldn't hurt a ruddy fly! They're all right. Nice lot o' kids, very trusting and as for the Commander—cor! he was dead easy."

He looked round to see whether his words had any softening affect on his captors.

"Look!" he protested. "What I done I done for us all. Share and share alike—all except him"— he nodded in the direction of Tom Huntingdon—"of course!"

Fatso fingered his seventh chin. "You can doublecross all the people some of the time," he said, "you can even doublecross some of the people all of the time : but you can't doublecross *all* of the people *all* of the time. That's what Abe Lincoln said and that goes for me too."

"Too right", said Cobbo. "Just sit yourself down where you are, Mister, while we decide what to do with you."

Pedro fingered his knife. "Not to trust such a man", he said. "What you think, Mister Tom?"

Tom was amazed. These men were on his side! After only three days they'd decided to throw their lot in with him. Or so it appeared.

Keeping his face in its best poker-playing expression he said, "I don't think you would be interested in my ideas.

You see I don't altogether hold with thieves. That man has stolen their boat and my ambergris. I'm definitely in favour of returning stolen properties to their rightful owners. But," he went on, "I'm an interested party and definitely old-fashioned where it comes to the difference between Meum and Tuum."

"Come again?" said Fatso.

"Sorry", said Tom. "That's Latin for 'what's mine is mine and what's yours is yours'."

Jeff Hooker spat on the groud in disgust. "What's come over you guys?" he demanded. "After all I've done for you—you act like a lot of sissies—letting him spout Latin at you. And another thing! Why did you let him make that signal? It nearly jiggered up the works. Are you all gone nuts?'

Pedro crept up to him. "Suppose you not talk so much, all right?" He touched his knife thoughtfully. Then he turned to Tom again. "You talk, Mister. What you say we do?"

"Well", said Tom. "I see it this way. You seem well disposed towards me and I appreciate that. This object here"—he nodded in the direction of Jeff Hooker—"has brought that yacht over to fetch us all back to Palmelo island. That was very thoughtful of him, but I've a feeling that if he could have managed without you, he'd have done so. And may yet do so at a later date. We'll avail ourselves of his thoughtfulness and sail back to the island. In return for your kindness to me I am prepared to share the proceeds of the ambergris with you three but on one condition—that man stays here!"

Jeff leapt to his feet. "You wouldn't do that to me!" he protested.

"You've just done it to my friend, the Commander," said

Tom, "and I will certainly do it to you if these gentlemen agree to it."

"Sure," said Fatso, "what's four into fifteen thousand?"

"Three and a half grand." Cobbo almost sang the words. "That's a lot of money!"

"There is, of course, a small contra," said Tom blandly: "your poker-debts Cobbo, remember?"

Cobbo swallowed hard. "You're a cool one," he said: "What do I owe you?"

"Getting on for just about that amount", said Tom. "And you too, Fatso."

Fatso grinned. "Fair's fair", he said.

Pedro looked sad. "How about me?" he asked.

Tom shook his head. "You would insist on doubling the stakes," he said. "But I tell you what—we'll cancel the whole thing and I'll give you each a thousand when I've sold the stuff—*if* I succeed in selling it. There are a lot of dishonest people in these parts."

"Too right", said Cobbo, looking at Jeff.

"You know somep'n?" said Fatso: "I never run across an honest guy before—it's a very strange feeling." He turned to Jeff Hooker: "you ought to try it some time, Jeff."

"Yes", said Pedro. "When dis guy Mister Tom say somep'n he just mean it. Glory Alleluia! No man ever talk me that way before. Seven year I in prison here. Dis Jeff Hooker mos' likely he land us all in the Pokey again the way he goes on. Stealing no way to carry on. Pedro in favour of Mister Tom."

"Too right", said Cobbo. "Me too."

"That makes it anonymous", said Fatso with more enthusiasm than literary accuracy. "That's how it is, Jeff! You ditched us so we ditch you. So long, Pal!"

Jeff stood helpless, a picture of baffled rage.

179

Tom got into the dinghy and the others pushed her into deep water before climbing aboard.

"I'll be even with you for this——" began Jeff Hooker and then broke into string after string of profanity.

"He'll be all right", said Tom. "The Tuna fishing fleet will be in any day now. If he talks nicely to them they'll give him a lift back to Mexico."

"Ah!" said Cobbo. "So that was it, was it? That was something he should have read about. What you said: 'if you want to know the future look in the past'."

"That's right", said Tom. The dinghy bumped alongside *Rag Doll* and they piled aboard her.

"So you was sitting pretty, all the time", said Cobbo.

"Me?" said Tom. "Oh yes, I was all right, and so were you, but I wasn't so sure about my friends. Let's get away from here and back to the island, just in case Mister Hooker thinks of swimming out. I wouldn't like him to do that the way the sharks are round here."

They soon found how to start *Rag Doll*'s diesel. Then they weighed anchor and set course to another part of the island.

"Tomorrow as soon as it's light," said Tom, "we'll go to Palmelo and hand her over to the Commander. And won't he be glad to see us!"

He remembered saying that when the first stone hurled by Mary hit him on the nose.

Chapter Twenty-Six

PEACE AND GOODWILL

CHRISTMAS DAY came fine and warm. The dawn
chorus of birds and beasts brought the humans out into
the sunshine at an early hour. Out at sea the water was
alive and sparkling as great shoals of fish jumped in a sort of
mad game of ring-a-roses.

"Tuna", said Tom. "Bang on time, as usual." He
climbed out of the dinghy on to *Rag Doll*'s deck where Uncle
George and his crew were waiting to receive him and his
three henchmen.

The two days which had elapsed since the "Battle of
Palmelo", as they had called it, had wrought great changes
in the physical appearances of the "Three Musketeers".
Gone were their straggling whiskers, ragged hair and dirty
clothing. With the aid of Mary's sewing-machine and an old
light weather sail Pedro, who had been taught elementary
tailoring during his enforced stay in the Galapagos, had
knocked up three pairs of jumpers and trousers. Fatso,
whose garments were a little on the tight side looked like an
overgrown baby. His chins were pink and shiny; his bald pate
gleamed in the sunshine and his little pig-like eyes had ceased
to peer suspiciously around him. He was at peace with the
world. So was Pedro, who had waxed his moustache so that
they projected some considerable distance on either side of his
face. His usual matted black hair was shining with grease
which he had removed from Tom Huntingdon's frying-pan
for the purpose. He came aboard speaking pure Spanish

in a voice which suggested nothing but goodwill and con-
gratulations. As for Cobbo, he always had been a picturesque figure. Tall and lean with a deeply-lined face, he
looked a typical out-back sheepman from Australia, which
he might have been if he had wished. Now, in his clean duck-
suit and a carelessly knotted red rag round his neck he could
have walked straight into a film studio and stolen the picture
from Gary Cooper himself.

Tom Huntingdon was his usual self, except for a large
piece of plaster on his nose—the only visible casualty of the
"battle". He greeted Uncle George with affectionate gaiety
and wished everybody the compliments of the season.
Presents were exchanged; cigarettes for the visitors from *Rag
Doll*'s nearly depleted stocks, and lumps of ambergris from
Fatso, Cobbo and Pedro who had scoured the beaches
during the previous day and now handed over their gifts in
a manner which reminded Uncle George of school-children
bringing an apple for the teacher.

When the presentations had been made Uncle George
told Ben to strike the bell for Church.

The dulcet notes of the silver ship's-bell sounded pure and
sweet; the strangely assorted congregation were transported
in their own minds to places where they had spent other
Christmases. So it has always been and so it will always be.
Away over the other side of the world were their relatives and
friends and soon they would all be linked together by a
voice, that of Her Majesty the Queen who was going to speak
as usual to all the people in the world who wanted to listen
to her.

"Fifteen minutes to go", said Uncle George. He opened
his prayer-book and read a few short prayers. Then they sang
some carols, with Loopy providing the music with his mouth-
organ. The singing wasn't very successful, for the visitors

didn't know the words but they made up for this by their enthusiasm for harmony.

Presently Uncle George turned the switch of the radio set to full power and the sonorous notes of Big Ben's chimes went out over the still waters until they reached the cliffs and sent back echoes; and as they did so the great sea-lions bellowed a chorus of welcome and clouds of birds rose from their niches in the cliffs as if aware of the importance of the occasion. Then came—"This is London!" To most of the listeners so many thousands of miles away, these words meant a great deal and even Pedro and Fatso who owed no allegiance to that part of the world felt the strong pull of the distant voice. Then came the sound of a woman's voice, simple, sweet and unaffected, reminding them of their kinship and wishing them all a Happy Christmas.

As the programme was ending with the National Anthem the spell of it all was rudely broken by the raucous sound of a ship's hooter. Uncle George turned to see a small Motor Patrol Boat rounding the point. Colonel Gaspardo was arriving at last!

Tom Huntingdon was the first to realise that the happy atmosphere of Christmas might be rudely shattered if Gaspardo sighted his visitors who had arrived at Palmelo without permission.

"Down below!" he hissed. The three men needed no further urging. They knew that if they were found they would spend the rest of their Christmas Day in goal, and probably a good many weeks after that before being repatriated in an uncomfortable manner to South America. Colonel Gaspardo would not hesitate to lock them up.

"Quick!" said Mary, as she led the way to the forepeak where all the sails were stowed. "In there," she ordered, "and spread the canvas over you just in case he searches."

It was a tight squeeze when Fatso joined the other two but they managed to get the door shut and as they did so they heard the sound of the Patrol Boat's engines as she was brought alongside *Rag Doll*.

Colonel Gaspardo was in his best uniform. Judging by the number of medals he was wearing he had been a very gallant soldier in his younger days, and unsuitable though they were he was still wearing his spurs.

"Greetings to all my friends", he called. "The happiest of Christmases to you all!"

"Come aboard!" replied Uncle George, "and have a glass of wine?" The Colonel once more executed a sort of step-dance as his spurs caught in the guard-rails, but this time he saved himself and made a more dignified arrival aboard. Saluting gravely he turned to the skipper of the Motor Patrol Boat and spoke fiercely in Spanish. Then with a different expression he spoke to Tom Huntingdon.

"So you have found your friend Commander Firebrace and his Blue Sailors?"

"Green", corrected Binnie automatically.

"Ah yes—Green! And you are having a good holiday together, yes?"

"Yes, indeed", said Tom.

"And no disturbings, eh?" The Colonel's eyes were bright and sharp.

"Such as?" drawled Tom.

"Such as Jeff Hookers?" said the Colonel. "My intelligence tells me of these matters."

Uncle George took the bottle of wine which Mary passed up and filled some glasses which he handed round. The Colonel bowed and shook his head.

"It is not good to drink wine under this sun," he said: "but downstairs yes—if you would be so kind."

There was nothing for it but to lead the way. As he entered the saloon the Colonel looked suspiciously round him. He sensed a feeling of tenseness aboard. Something told him that these people were not being entirely open with him. When he was seated he repeated, "such as Jeff Hookers?"

The three men huddled in the forepeak could hear every word. They held their breaths as they waited for the answer, for they were mighty afraid that these honest people might not feel inclined to tell a lie on their behalf.

"Jeff Hooker?" replied Uncle George, "where have I heard that name before?"

Tom smiled. "Colonel Gaspardo is convinced that Jeff Hooker will come to this island for nefarious reasons—is that not so, Colonel?"

"Certainly", said the Colonel. "My intelligences cannot be at fault. I have evidence that his ship was sighted only a few days' sail from this place."

"How long ago?" asked Tom.

"A week—ten days?" said the Colonel.

"Then he should be here by now", said Tom.

"Indeed yes", said Uncle George.

"Have you searched the coasts? Ships can't disappear."

"This one has", said the Colonel.

"Very strange", said Uncle George.

"You have not seen another ship?"

It was Uncle George who was able to answer truthfully. "Not a sausage", he replied.

"Ah," said the Colonel, "I am very fond of sausage—you have some?"

Mary went to a locker and produced a tin. "For Christmas", she said.

At that moment Fatso gave a prodigious sneeze. "What was that?" demanded the Colonel.

"Polly-the-Parrot", said Ben quickly. "She's always pretending to sneeze—aren't you, Polly?"

Polly gave him a dirty look. "Aw! drop dead", she said in her best imitation of Loopy's voice, and then to everyone's horror she added: "Jeff Hooker! Jeff Hooker!"

The Colonel roared with laughter. "You sell me that bird?" he said wiping his eyes: "how much?"

Uncle George shook his head.

"Perhaps she will sneeze again?"

"Not if you look at her", said Ben.

"Another glass of wine, Colonel?" said Uncle George.

"Ta—ta—thank you, Senor." He held out his glass as Fatso gave another tremendous sneeze. "Wonderful!" said the Colonel. "So like life! I shall buy a bird like that. With such a one—no need to have a gramophone. Yes?"

He drained his glass and rose to go.

"There is one thing that might throw some light on your investigations, Colonel", said Tom Huntingdon. "Over on Little Palmelo I've noticed some smoke recently. Perhaps the people you are looking for are camping there?"

"But where is their ship?" said the Colonel.

"Search me!" said Tom.

"Very droll", said Colonel Gaspardo. "I search you for a ship, eh? You fonny man, Mister Huntingdon. And now —when do you leave Galapagos, Commander?"

"There are many islands to visit," said Uncle George, "and we are in no hurry."

"Very well", said the Colonel drawing a rubber date-stamp from his capacious pockets. Give me your passport and I will stamp it now. How's that?"

Another prodigious sneeze. The Colonel looked at the Parrot. "It is miraculous," he said, "if I had not heard it myself I would have sworn it came from there!" He pointed towards the bows.

The three musketeers held their breaths. Cobbo had Fatso's nose between his fingers and thumb and Pedro's knife was being waved before his eyes.

Bang! went the rubber stamp. The Colonel waited.

"She won't sneeze to order", said Uncle George.

"Then I wait to see it."

"As you wish", said Uncle George nonchalantly. Things were getting a bit dicey.

"Another glass of wine?" he suggested.

"Thank you, Senor."

Uncle groaned inwardly. Mary and Mark sent up a mute prayer for deliverance from this intolerable situation. It was answered almost at once. A loud-hailer could be heard wishing everybody a Merry Christmas.

"It is Bernardino and the Tuna fishing-fleet at last!" cried Tom. "Come, Colonel and give them your official welcome and don't forget, he who answers first is given the best Tuna!"

The Colonel rose, looked resentfully at Polly and went on deck. As he left the saloon Fatso almost exploded. The Colonel heard it. "That is not a nice bird," he said, "no proper behavings."

There were seventeen Tuna-boats, great rust-streaked vessels which had started life as schooners and now depended upon powerful diesels to push them along. They came honking into the bay and dropped their anchors all round *Rag Doll*. This was to be a day of rest and rejoicing before the fleet started work in the morning. The people aboard these vessels were a jolly lot and when they saw the shoals of jumping fish they became even jollier, for they knew then

that the harvest was ready for the taking and their liveli-
hood was assured for the next twelve months.

Bernardino came over in his dory and after saluting the
Colonel and handing him a paper containing all particulars
of his ship and those who accompanied her, turned to embrace Tom Huntingdon.

"You see, Senor!" he exclaimed. "Bernardino does not
forget!"

Colonel Gaspardo studied the documents with undis-
guised disgust. Clearly they were in perfect order and there
was nothing to do but stamp them. Out came the ink-pad
and rubber stamp and that was that. He clambered back
aboard the Patrol Boat and ordered her skipper to go.

"You will inspect the other island?" asked Tom.

The Colonel shrugged. "Maybe yes," he said: "but not
until the Fiesta is finished. Christmastide is not for work, but
if you should see the *Black Jack* or those Jeff Hookers you
will intelligent me, please?"

"Certainly", said Uncle George. "A very Merry Christmas, Colonel."

"And the same with nobs on", came the elegant reply.

"For you," called Bernardino, "I will bring a fine Tuna!"

And so with the best of good wishes all round Colonel
Gaspardo went away, leaving *Rag Doll* and her new-found
friends to spend the day together in harmony. And harmony
was the right word, for Bernardino and his fellow fishermen
were masters when it came to dance music.

Uncle George and his crew were bidden aboard the *Vera
Cruz* for an evening of entertainment and they accepted the
invitation with alacrity. Before this took place, however,
Tom went back with Bernardino for a private talk with him
and returned to say that all had been arranged. Fatso, Pedro
and Cobbo were released from their cramped quarters and

informed that Bernardino had agreed to sign them on as extra fishermen to help in the very strenuous work of tuna-fishing, in return for which he would take them back to the mainland and see that they were allowed to go ashore without trouble with the police. Bernardino had also agreed to transport the cargo of ambergris *and* Tom Huntingdon himself back to Mexico. The tuna catch would only take a few days and the *Vera Cruz* would then start the long voyage home. "So," ordered Tom, "if and when Colonel Gaspardo gets round to paying Jeff Hooker a visit and persuades him to talk there will be no danger that the Colonel will be able to lock up his former associates."

Cobbo spoke for the remainder: "I said you was a cool one," he said, "from the very first I said it. You're real bonzer, chum!"

Pedro echoed his praises in his own way.

"If any man try to steal your ambergris," he said, "I, Pedro, will personally cut his t'roat!"

Fatso began to make a speech about the unity of the Anglo-Saxon-speaking nations with large quotations from Abraham Lincoln, but a fresh fit of sneezing reduced everybody to howls of laughter and he was obliged to subside into a sulky silence, punctuated by a last few sporadic explosions.

So it was all agreed.

Nobody aboard *Rag Doll* will ever forget that Christmas night aboard Bernardino's ship. Large as she was the *Vera Cruz* was a foot lower in the water for the weight of people aboard her. They sat in rows and sang incomprehensible songs in the strange harmony of their race. Then, one after the other they rose to dance, sometimes in pairs, sometimes singly and sometimes in a wild melange of snapping castanets

and strumming guitars. And when there was not music
and dancing there were acrobatics. The fishermen were
very strong—they had to be for the work they did. Now they
exhibited their strength with pyramids of bodies held up by a
single man.

Fatso soon settled in, though unable to understand a word
they said to him. From his pocket he produced three walnut
shells and a single pea and before long he was persuading the
simple fisherfolk to play a little game with him. They had to
guess under which shell the pea was, and when they found
how easy it was they were persuaded to follow Cobbo's
example and put a silver dollar by the shell which they
fancied to contain the pea. Cobbo won six times running and
was persuaded to double his stake, but when the fishermen
tried somehow they were not so successful and as the evening
wore on Fatso's pockets began to bulge and clink.

It was all like a sort of fair and circus combined—the
music went on and on, the fishermen drank raw wine and
became merrier and merrier, and as the ships' bells rang out
eight times for midnight the Greens suddenly felt very very
tired. Quietly, so as not to break up the festivities they and
the others departed in their boats and went back to *Rag Doll*.
Long after they'd turned in the sounds of festivity echoed in
their dreams. The fisherfolk were making a night of it—but
when the day broke they were all at sea, hooking in the great
tuna—hard and ceaseless work which went on till dark.
Then back they came to anchor in the bay and once again
the music came over the water with a strange and haunting
beauty. But not from Fatso, Pedro and Cobbo! They were
completely exhausted and, said Bernardino, who came over
for a drink and a yarn with Uncle George—they would be
too stiff to work in the morning. As for Tom, he had spent
the day ashore packing up his belongings and specimens.

The fisherfolk were making a night of it.

On the third day of Christmas so great had the fish-harvest been that all the Tuna-boats were fully loaded. One tremendous evening of rejoicing ensued. Every fisherman was convinced that this extraordinary draught of Tuna was somehow connected with the presence of *Rag Doll*. They pressed round the visitors to touch them for luck, and then as the full moon reached its zenith the final good-byes were said and the *Rag Doll*'s crew stayed up to watch their departure.

One after the other the boats came close past the yacht, their crews singing the traditional "farewell and adieu" of their country. Steadily they went by and set course to pass out of sight beyond the distant headland; the beat of their engines and the honking of their exhausts lingered long after they were out of sight. Presently new noises came to the listeners' ears—the squealing of rats, the chirping of crickets and tree-frogs which had been submerged by the raucous sound of human rejoicing now returned to take possession of Palmelo Island—once more uninhabited. The birds, beasts, reptiles and insects were now in undisputed possession and it was time for *Rag Doll* to move on. The place seemed lonely and desolate now that the others were gone with their ambergris and high hopes of a better life in the future.

As for Jeff Hooker, they had a glimpse of him aboard Colonel Gaspardo's patrol-boat which came nosing into the bay only a few hours after the fleet had sailed. True to his despicable self Jeff had informed against his former shipmates, but too late!

Colonel Gaspardo was not pleased and showed his displeasure by turning his back on *Rag Doll*'s crew who waved a cheerful greeting.

Clearly, said Uncle George, it was time for them to be moving on in search of fresh adventures and new people. The world was a large place—there was much more to be seen and met with and time was slipping away.

Many more days were spent in the Galapagos before *Rag Doll* set out to cross the mighty Pacific. There further adventures must await another volume before they can be told.

THE END

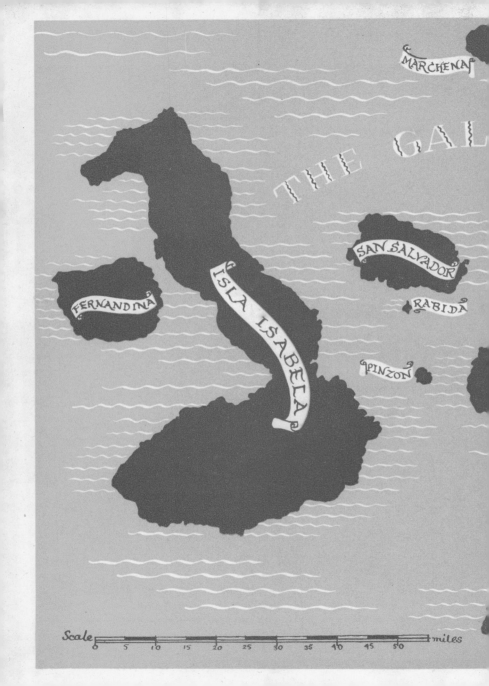